Lust hit Jake like a brick; quick, hard and ruthless. A decade of pent-up desire and sexual frustration sent him to the floor—to his knees. Transfixed with the pale brown skin of her breasts, he prayed for the strength not to touch her. Prayed that she would wake up before he succumbed. Yet she slept.

He was mesmerized by the rise and fall of the soft, round mounds as she breathed, and even more intrigued by the trail of tiny tears on one perfect breast. Not real tears, he noted, but tattoos that began at the rise of her breast and slid into the dark crevice where her breasts met.

Indigo Sensuous Love Stories

are published by

Genesis Press, Inc.
315 Third Avenue North
Columbus, MS 39701
www.genesis-press.com

Copyright©2002 by Tanya T. Henderson

Tattooed Tears

First Edition

Tattooed Tears

by
T.T. Henderson

Genesis Press, Inc.

DEDICATION

To the gang of "cubicle dwellers" who inspired the title of this novel and kept me going through the toughest of times, your old Jefé thinks the world of you and thanks you very much.

Chapter One

Shay Bennett believed in the power of prayer, the freedom of being an American, the addictive power of a man's kiss and love that never died.

All her beliefs had been shattered on one pristinely beautiful day.

America had been attacked by terrorists and was at war. Even three months after the attack it was hard to reconcile, harder still to get through each day without the man she loved. Instead of getting on with her life, she seemed to be standing still, stalled by mounting regrets.

"I should've kissed him." Shay examined the bottle in her hand for a long, tortured moment. "Just once," she whispered, swirling the remaining liquid around the bottle, knowing this wasn't the answer to her problems. Knew it. But what else was there? Her prayers hadn't been answered; her misery hadn't eased. One painful day blended into another as she threw herself into her work during the day and sat transfixed before the television each evening. Any day, she'd prayed, any day they would find Jerome, and by some miracle, he'd be alive.

"All those prayers." She slurred words as she gulped down wine she no longer tasted. "And they can't even find his body to give him a proper funeral."

Unsteadily, she placed the bottle to her lips, tipped back her head and let the last of the blood red Merlot choke its way down her throat. Shay dropped the empty bottle onto the floor next to her. It rolled back and forth over the newspaper she'd left there. Jerome's soot-blackened face was on the front page, looking determined as he raced down Canal Street. A crying woman lay weak in his arms, her dress torn, one shoe missing, the smoke and debris of Ground Zero billowing in the background. The headline read, "Heroism rises despite Twin Towers' fall."

The article told of how stockbroker Jerome Masters had vacated his office on the 32nd floor of the first Twin Tower prior to its fall, but had gone back to pull person after person from the rubble as others fled the scene. The woman in his arms had been the last saved before Jerome had gone back inside never to return.

Shay had been in love with Jerome ever since she could remember. But she should have known things between them would end like this—some other woman being the one to feel his last embrace. It was probably her own fault. She'd never let him know how she truly felt about him. But it was hard to take that step and potentially ruin a lifetime of friendship.

They'd played together within the courtyard of their low-rent housing complex when they were children. She'd cried when he'd gone to the prom with Fast Annie instead of her, and when he'd received a scholarship to play football at New York University while she had to attend a junior college. They'd been roommates for the past ten years, sharing rent on an expensive flat in downtown New York. They'd fallen into an easy friendship, lived comfortably together, but rarely saw each other. Jerome loved parties and spontaneous trips to anywhere. Shay liked quiet evenings at home.

She'd cooked for him, washed his clothes and cleaned his room. He'd always told her not to, that it wasn't necessary. It had always surprised her when he'd wash the dishes, mop the floor or clean the bathroom on weekends when he had nowhere to go.

It had been perfect except for one thing. Shay had it bad for him, and Jerome had been totally clueless. Jerome loved women. Loved the look of them, the smell of them, the many colors of them. All of them…except her. Instead of searing looks of lust, he looked at her as if she were his sister. Instead of sneaking into her bedroom at night for a little loving, he'd come in to talk about his latest woman woes over hot cocoa or green tea.

Shay had listened, and advised as best as she could with an unwilling heart. He'd talk and she'd long for the sweet taste of his lips to land on her mouth instead of her forehead. She dreamed of being bold enough to wear revealing nightgowns instead flannel pajamas in his presence. She died a thousand deaths each time he found a new woman to warm his bed.

As long as he never married, Shay thought, there was a chance for them. She'd pray every day for the man to love her the way she loved him.

"And now, it's too late," she whined, dropping her chin to her chest. Her head throbbed madly. It had for weeks. Ever since the memorial service. Ever since she'd heard his name called by the minister and watched his mother weep.

Shay's eyes grew heavy, as did the rest of her body. Sleep. That's what she needed. A good night's sleep would keep the hurt away for a few hours. *Was* it night? she wondered. It was so hard to tell on Saturdays.

Feeling sleepier than she'd ever felt, she moved a heavy

arm to grasp the bottle of pain reliever. Only two pills remained. Could that be right? She thought she had more.

Didn't matter. Shay attempted to shove them between her lips. One, then the other threatened to fall to the floor.

She managed to swallow them down dry. Shoving aside the newspaper and wine bottle, Shay lay on the rug and curled herself into a ball. Her head pounded worse from the effort for a bit, then began to subside. Sleep. That's all she needed. Sleep.

Jacob Masters stood before the door, studying the forest green paint, wondering for the hundredth time in an hour if this was the right thing to do. Exhaling hard, he shook his head. "This is stupid," he said, shuffling his feet. He should just walk in. This was his home. Had been anyway.

Jake fit the key into the lock, a little surprised that it slid in so easily. The lock hadn't been changed. That was something.

His fist closed over the knob and he froze. What if he wasn't welcome? What then? He knew that when surprised, Jerome was more prone to fighting than discussing.

Releasing the knob, Jake pulled the key out, closed a fist around it and shoved it back into his pocket. The worst thing he could do was provoke a fight with his brother. After all, he needed somewhere to live. At least until he figured out what living was again.

He knocked hard and waited. He turned his ear toward the door but could hear no movement on the other side. He knocked two more times before telling himself the obvious. His brother wasn't home.

"Damn," he said quietly. This was going to be difficult enough. The last thing he'd wanted was to have to sit here and wait on him, but what choice did he have? There was nowhere else to go. Once again, he removed the key from his pocket and slid it inside the lock. This time he opened the door and stepped inside.

It was different. Very different from when he'd left. There were watercolor paintings on the walls now. Peach walls, he noted. An expensive looking multi-colored wool rug and dining room furniture filled the space between the living room and kitchen instead of the card table and folding chairs he and Jerome used to have.

Jake's heart raced as he thought the unthinkable. What if someone else lived here now? Maybe Jerome had moved. Panic numbed his limbs and his mind. He couldn't think. If he was caught here...

A low moan came from the direction of the couch. He

spotted someone lying on the floor in front of it. Jake could tell it was a woman, even though he could see only her feet. He reached for the doorknob and missed on his first try. Sweat broke out on his forehead as he struggled to catch his breath. He couldn't be caught in here...couldn't go back.

As he opened the door, the woman called out, "Jerome? Is that you?"

Relief came as the familiar name was spoken. Maybe she was one of Jerome's girlfriends. Nothing to worry about. "No. Not Jerome," he answered, trying to catch his breath.

But the woman didn't respond further. Only lay there, her bare feet peeking past the edge of the overstuffed couch. His couch, Jake realized. The one he and his brother had purchased more than ten years ago. Only the pillows on the couch were new and bright with color.

Curious, Jake walked around to face the woman. She was sleeping, her brown hair with golden highlights spiraling in an explosion of ringlets fell haphazardly upon her soft milky-brown features. A sprinkling of light brown freckles danced across the bridge of her nose and cheeks. Her ethnic features and sandy brown coloring indicated that she was mixed white and black.

It hit him then. He knew her. It was Shay. Shay from the

projects. Only she'd done a lot of growing up since he'd last seen her. His eyes roamed over her curves covered loosely by a flannel robe. From where he stood, he could see the absolute perfection of her cleavage where the robe fell open—and it was his undoing.

Lust hit Jake like a brick; quick, hard and ruthless. A decade of pent-up desire and sexual frustration sent him to the floor—to his knees. Transfixed with the pale brown skin of her breasts, he prayed for the strength not to touch her. Prayed that she would wake up before he succumbed. Yet she slept.

He was mesmerized by the rise and fall of the soft, round mounds as she breathed, and even more intrigued by the trail of tiny tears on one perfect breast. Not real tears, he noted, but tattoos that began at the rise of her breast and slid into the dark crevice where her breasts met.

Closing his eyes, Jake strained to think of something else. Lusting after Shay Bennett was like drooling over his sister. After all, he and Jerome had been her defenders as they grew up together. Seemed like Shay was always letting her mouth write checks her skinny body couldn't cash. His now open eyes scanned the sexy curve of her hips as the flannel hugged them. Skinny wasn't exactly how he'd describe her now.

"What's wrong with you, Jake?" he whispered to himself. Having a woman should be the last thing knocking about in his addled brain. It was a woman who'd made him lose ten years of his life. A woman he vowed to have a reckoning with as soon as possible. Old bitterness and anger eased his erection—slightly.

To get his mind off sex, Jake scanned the floor around Shay. An empty Tylenol bottle, a wine bottle in the same condition, and a newspaper.

Had she tried to kill herself on alcohol and Tylenol? No, he decided. She looked too peaceful—her breathing too regular. Although it looked like she'd attempted to drown her sorrows. He lifted the wine bottle and stood it upright on the coffee table. His eyes fell to the newspaper lying just under her hand. The face on the front page—a mirror image of his own—shot a strong sense of dread deep inside him. As he allowed his eyes to fall to the text, his vision blurred. He knew that what he would see there would be bad. Very bad.

Jake's mouth went dry as he forced a trembling hand toward the paper. Slowly, carefully, he slid the paper close enough to read the headline, then the story.

Tears he'd never cried for himself now forced themselves out of Jake's tightly shut eyes. "No," he cried. "No."

Cries that were not her own crept into Shay's troubled sleep, waking her. Groggy from the potency of Merlot heartache, she found it difficult to open her eyes. But the next wail of grief forced them open and sent her whole body on alert.

A man sat hunched into a tight ball, rocking forward and back as if suffering from a blow to his gut.

Shay pushed from the floor onto unsteady legs. "Who are you? Why are you here?" she asked, clasping her robe around her and grabbing the wine bottle by its neck.

The man uncurled enough to face her.

His face...Shay was confused. "Jerome? How did you...I thought you were..."

The man shook his head, wiped the tears from his face briskly. "It's me, Shay. Jake."

"Jake?" Jake was in jail, practically for life. "Why are you teasing me?" she asked. "I've been so worried about you, Jerome." She went to stand before him, hesitated, then threw her arms around his neck. "I thought I'd never get the chance to kiss you." With that, she pressed her lips to his. At first unyielding, Jake then parted his lips and pushed his tongue inside her mouth.

It was like heat and light running through Shay at once.

His arms were strong as they pulled her in close against the solid muscles of his chest. It was just as she'd imagined it would be—only better. She hadn't counted on his wanting her just as much as she wanted him, but his lips and tongue and hands were seeking, probing and pressing with more urgency. His moans were long and low and made Shay weak-kneed and euphoric. She was lost. So lost. "Take me, Jerome. Please take me," she offered as he pressed hot, hungry kisses down her neck. There would be no restraint this time. She would make the most of this second chance. There would be no more regrets.

His hands moved inside her robe and caressed her waist and hips and then stopped. "Shay," his voice was thick and shaky. "Cover yourself, Shay. Please."

Confusion forced Shay's eyes open. Embarrassment had her closing her robe and dropping her head. "I'm sorry, Jerome—"

"No." He put a hand on her arm, then quickly removed it. "Look at me, Shay," he instructed.

God, she didn't want to. She'd rather be struck dead right now, but she forced herself to meet his eyes. Eyes that were deeply brown were set in the hard lines of his striking medium-brown features. He bit his bottom lip, forcing his cheeks to dimple.

Then, she saw the truth. He was absolutely gorgeous, but he wasn't Jerome. Though identical twins, Jerome and Jake had some distinguishing characteristics. Jake had a slightly leaner face, and deeper dimples than Jerome. Only people who were close to them could ever tell the difference. "Jake?" she asked with even more embarrassment.

He nodded, his eyes softened with apology.

"Wow." Shay pushed her springy curls back off her face and pulled her robe closer around her. Backing up, she tried to think of what to say to make this situation less awkward. "I thought you were Jerome," she offered by way of explanation.

"Yeah." Jake shifted from one foot to the other. "I got that."

"Well, if you understood that, why did you let me..." She gestured helplessly as she searched for the right words. "You know!"

"Don't be mad." The eyes so like Jerome's looked at her longingly. "It's been a long time since I've touched a woman."

"So you thought you'd take advantage of the situation?" Shay *was* mad now. "Why are you here?"

Jake looked down at the newspaper clutched in his hand, now damp with his tears. "I came to see...to see Jerome. I was..." He swallowed hard, as if the words were clogging his throat. His striking features twitched and distorted violently as he pressed his fingers to his eyes. Distress filled Shay. She'd never seen a grown man cry before. At least not right in front of her. What was she supposed to do? To say? After three months she still couldn't find words to comfort herself.

"I'm so sorry," was all she could manage. Approaching him with small, hesitant steps, she struggled to find more words of comfort.

Jake's shoulders shook as his sobbing intensified. Cautiously, Shay reached out a hand, intending to pat his back.

Jake threw both arms around her waist and clung to her as if she were a life raft in a storm-tossed sea.

The man's grip was like a vice around her mid-section. She didn't know how to tell him without hurting his feelings. Of course, if he made her robe any wetter with his crying...or worse yet, if his nose started to run... "Jake." Attempting to wiggle from his grip, she pushed at solidly muscled arms.

"Sorry," he said, loosening his grip.

"I have tissue." Shay, grateful for her freedom, grabbed the box of Kleenex from the table and offered it to him. "I'd offer you Merlot if I had any more."

When Jake looked up into her face, a smile took hold of one corner of his lips.

"What?"

"You haven't changed a bit," he said, shaking his head. "You never were much on tears, were you, Shay? As I recall, you'd rather fight than cry. Heck, you'd rather do anything than cry."

Shrugging, Shay backed up a little. "Tears never got me anywhere." She wanted to say that she considered them to be a sign of weakness, but didn't want to hurt his feelings. "'cept a beatin' for waking my mom up."

Jake nodded as if he recalled hearing her screams through the paper-thin walls between their old apartments. "It's good to see you again," he added quietly.

"Yeah, you too." Not certain that she meant it, Shay moved back to sit on the sofa. Having him here was so confusing all of a sudden. "Have a seat."

Jake selected the extra wide chair opposite to where she sat, moving the ottoman to the side. He wiped at his eyes and nose and waited, knowing she had questions.

"I didn't know you were getting out." Shay sat back on the couch and pulled her hands through her wild brown ringlets. "Did Jerome know?"

"Not for sure," he stated. "Last time I saw him, I told him I had my lawyer request DNA testing to prove my innocence. I wasn't sure when they'd be able to get the testing done. But it proved I didn't do it."

"You're no rapist," Shay said firmly. "Jerome and I both know that. Knew that," she corrected. "I'm surprised Jerome didn't tell me, though." Shay shook her head. "When did you see him?"

"Back in August."

"So nobody told you what happened to him? You didn't see the paper? It's been three months now."

"I got a message that Jerome called me on his cell phone as soon as he evacuated the building. He knew I'd be worried since he worked in the Towers." Jake ran a tired hand over his face. "He asked the authorities to tell me he was safe, and they did. It didn't occur to me to worry about him going back in."

"I watched CNN almost constantly for weeks, but I never saw a story about Jerome. All I heard about were the firemen and police officers who'd died. It consumed everyone in the pen for weeks. How did I miss this?"

"I can't believe your mother or sister didn't tell you."

Jake gave her a long, steady gaze. "You know Momma and Jenna disowned me when I was convicted," he challenged. "Actually," he shrugged, "they gave up on me before the trial was half over. I could see it in their eyes. There was no support for me in the end."

Shay noted that his face twisted in disgust at the memory. "Must be rough, having your own family lack faith in you."

"As I recall, your mother wasn't all that nurturing to you. Has that changed?"

"My mother's dead," Shay said matter-of-factly. It was hard to care. "Coroner wasn't sure if it was the bullet through her gut or the high dose of crack in her veins that did her in, but it really didn't matter. That was about three years ago."

"So now you're alone in the world, too."

Silence fell between them as each retreated to private thoughts. It was Shay who finally spoke again. "How did you get in? Did I forget to lock the door?"

Jake fished the key from his pocket and displayed it in his palm. "I was surprised it still worked."

"It was tough to find an apartment in the city back then.

Still is. Jerome needed someone to help with rent when you went to prison, I needed somewhere to live after I graduated from college…" She shrugged. "It worked out."

"In a strange twist of fate," Jake pocketed the key once more, "now I'm the one who needs some place to live. I was hoping Jerome would take me in until I could get back on my feet." Jake gave a pleading gesture. "Would you mind?"

"No," Shay said quickly, feeling obligated to do so. Finding a new roommate was one of the things she'd needed to do, but hadn't placed high on her priority list. She'd dipped into savings for the past couple of months to make the rent. She could continue to do so for a couple more months. "It's okay by me," she said. "I can carry the rent for a couple more months if necessary."

"Thanks," Jake said. "I have some money in savings, not much," he offered. "I was wiped out with trial expenses so all I have is what I earned while in prison."

"They pay you in jail?" Her eyes widened with surprise.

"Yeah. One of the rehab programs. It was either do tele-marketing or find religion. Since I was pissed off with God at the time, I chose telemarketing."

Not wanting to get into a subject as touchy as religion, given her shaken faith, Shay simply nodded and yawned simultaneously. "I'm completely wasted. I'm going to bed. You can take Jerome's room, if you like."

"All right." Jake watched her shuffle toward the room that used to be his.

Shay stood looking at the room. Her look was unreadable. "I haven't cleaned it or anything. I didn't want to touch Jerome's personal things...in case he came back."

"It's all right." Jake stood in the doorway next to her, dreading the thought of going in. He noted the cream-colored satin sheets entwined with a rich gold and black comforter. Jerome had never been much on making his bed; he'd insisted that it was only necessary to impress a woman visitor, but a waste of time otherwise. "Hell, you're just going to get back in it," he'd argued.

There were matching gold drapes topped by fancy black valances and half-burned candles strategically placed on furniture around the room. Everything about the room screamed *Player*.

"The room is just what I'd expect of Rome," Jake said, wondering how many women had been seduced in this room.

Without saying another word, Shay walked across the hallway to her own room and closed the door quietly.

Jake wondered just how much Shay had minded.

Sighing, he leaned against the doorjamb. It felt strange to be here. He could feel Jerome, smell him. If he looked hard enough, his brother would simply be there, standing before him—at least that's how he felt.

"Can you hear me, bro?" he asked warily. "I hope it's okay, me being here. I've got nowhere else to go." He gave an uneasy laugh and gestured wearily. "But you know that, huh?"

He listened for a reply that never came. "I guess it's a good thing," he said and entered the room, "that I can't hear you," he explained, taking a seat on the edge of the bed. "Means I'm not a lunatic or anything. I'd like to talk to you anyway...if that's all right."

Jake pinched back the threat of fresh tears with a thumb and forefinger to his eyes. "I thought the loneliest I would ever feel was in that damned jail cell, Rome. Thought I'd jump for joy when I got out."

His blurry eyes roamed the room aimlessly. "It's scarier out here than it ever was inside. Everything's new, different, you know? I don't know where to start...what to do. I needed you to help me, Rome. I need you."

Shay closed the door to her room quietly against the man's fresh sobs. She had intended to walk over and tell Jake he was welcome to anything in the kitchen. After overhearing his "conversation" she figured there'd be no use. He didn't sound like he'd be too hungry at the moment. Besides, his sobbing was disturbing.

She rounded her bed to stand at the window. There was nothing to see, as usual, which made it perfect. Staring at the weathered bricks across the alley helped her to think. But she didn't like the unpleasant thoughts popping into her head. He bugged her, Jake did. She'd never seen a man cry so much. It was understandable, she guessed. He *had* lost his twin brother. But her mother had taught her years ago, with the back of her hand, that tears would not be tolerated.

Maybe that was why Shay was uncomfortable with Jake's tears. Yet at the same time, she was tremendously attracted to him. Mistaken identity or not, she'd enjoyed his kisses, his hands roaming her back and behind. "But that's because you thought he was Jerome," she reminded herself.

It was ironic, this situation. Losing a man she couldn't get enough of and gaining one that she didn't know what to do with. All Shay knew was that Jacob Masters had better get his act together quickly. He made her uncomfortable on too many levels and Shay had had enough of discomfort.

Chapter Two

Jake opened his eyes to darkness. The clock on the bedside table flickered the time of 6:08 a.m. on beams of arced light that seemed to dance between the sides of the clock. Damnedest thing he'd ever seen. Besides that, there was no other light. No light outside the room to cast menacing shadows of bars inside his cell. Hell, there were no bars. No cell. No sounds of men's snoring, coughing, laughing, belching, cursing. No echoes of security guard footsteps down wide hallways.

And there were no familiar smells. Not the stifling odor of urine and antiseptic cleaners that normally filled his room. There was only the subdued sound of a shower running in the bathroom and traffic somewhere outside the apartment building.

He was free. He was supposed to be happy about that. Would've been if not for his brother being gone. Jake closed his eyes once again, rubbing a hand over his aching chest. All that crying yesterday had left his ribs and chest sore and his eyes feeling as if they'd been bathed in sandpaper.

Not the least of his discomfort was his full bladder. In prison, there had been a urinal inside each cell. Here, there was only one bathroom and Shay appeared to have taken out a month's lease on it. Jake doubted that she'd be overly thrilled in having him run in to relieve himself while she showered. The thought of her naked in the next room sent a flash of lust to his already uncomfortable loins.

Jake still didn't know how he'd found the strength to stop touching her the day before. The taste of her mouth was sweet and tart and she'd smelled of powder and flowers. Her skin had felt like warm satin beneath his hands. There was something so right about the feel of her in his arms...but he couldn't start out by betraying her trust. He needed her.

And he needed to use the bathroom.

She wouldn't be in there forever. Jake turned his mind to other things to ease his discomfort. He needed to find a job. Of course, he didn't know if he'd remember how to take the subway to get from here to anywhere but the prison, but he'd figure it out. Guess the first thing he needed would be the paper. Find out what was in the classifieds.

Satisfied with having a purpose, Jake rose from the bed, realizing that he'd slept with his clothes on, and that standing up made the pressure on his bladder even worse.

He sat back on the edge of the bed, but there was no relief. He cupped his hands over his crotch as if they could hold back the force of nature that seemed determined to happen sooner rather than later.

Thankfully, the shower stopped. Shay would be out any second now.

Standing up in anticipation, Jake began pacing circles in the room. "Come on, Shay. Come on, babe. I gotta go. Gotta go," he whispered desperately. Each second seemed like an hour. Maybe he should just tap on the door and tell her he needed to use the bathroom. Then again, he didn't want to rush her.

The newspaper, he thought. He'd go get the paper from the hallway and maybe she'd be out by then.

Awkwardly, he walked, hopped, and twisted his way to the front door. Carefully, he bent over to get the *Times* and closed the door behind him. His grip tightened on the paper as his bladder threatened to give. This whole diversion thing wasn't working.

Running to the kitchen, he threw open four cabinets before finding several sipper cups neatly aligned on the bottom shelf of one. "Thank you, God," he said in a pained whisper. Pulling the largest sipper cup from the shelf, Jake ripped off the lid, slid his zipper down, shoved his hand down his briefs and pulled out just in time to catch the hot, heavy urine as it flowed from him in a burst of pure desperation.

Jake laid back his head, closed his eyes and let out a long sigh of bliss as his bladder emptied and the cup he held grew heavy. He didn't believe he'd ever peed for so long before in his life. Finally, when there were just drops left, Jake opened his eyes only to meet the blazing brown of Shay Bennett's. She stared across the counter at him, hands on her hips.

Jake turned hot with embarrassment.

"That, Jacob Masters, is the most disgusting thing I've ever seen."

"Sorry, Shay…I didn't…it's just that you were in the bathroom for so long—" Jake put the cup on the counter and adjusted his pants.

"In case you haven't noticed, this is a home, not a prison. You can't just relieve yourself anywhere you please."

"No…I know—"

"If this is how you're going to behave, then I'm going to have to take back my offer of letting you stay."

"But, Shay—"

She disappeared into her room for a moment and came back with her coat and purse. "Leave your key on the counter and be gone by the time I get home tonight." With that, she put on her coat, yanked her purse over a shoulder, and was gone.

"Damn!" Jake struck the counter with his fist. "What the hell am I going to do now?"

❖

Olivia Masters sipped her coffee. It had gone cold some time ago, as she'd dozed, but she drank it anyway. It was too much effort to get up and microwave it back to an acceptable temperature. T.D. Jakes was preaching on the television that she always kept tuned to the Christian network. Normally, she hung on every word this preacher said, but not today. Not for a day-and-a-half. Not since she'd received the call from Jake's attorney, telling her that Jake had been given a DNA test and was found not to be the match for the man who'd raped a woman ten years ago. He was innocent. Always had been.

The knocking at her front door was insistent.

Please go away.

She knew it was his knocking that had awakened her. It was Jake at the door.

Olivia didn't move. She couldn't answer the door. Couldn't.

"Mama," his voice called from the other side of the door. "I know you're home, I can hear the TV. Let me in, please."

Olivia took another sip of cold coffee.

"I just wanna talk to you, Mama," he pleaded gently. "I need somewhere to stay."

Staring more intently at the television that sat on top of an old stereo console that hadn't worked for over a decade, Olivia tried to understand what the preacher was saying. His sermon wasn't making sense today. It was all just a jumble of words. "Mama. Please," he said.

But the words didn't match the movement of his lips. She had no idea what he was talking about. Soon the preaching stopped and he began to pray. Olivia closed her eyes, grateful that there was no more pleading. No more knocking.

A lonely tear slid down her face as she found she couldn't pray with the preacher. No words would come.

She let the coffee cup slide from her hands. It shattered on the wood floor, cold coffee staining her old rug. But it didn't matter. Nothing mattered anymore.

Olivia covered her face with her hands—covered her shame.

Jake turned away from the door. A cold wind whipped down the street. Throwing the hood of his brother's coat over his head, he walked back toward the subway. He had no idea how to find his sister Jenna. Jerome had said she'd gotten married about five years ago and had a couple of kids now. She lived somewhere in Jersey, but that was no help. There were a lot of "somewheres" in Jersey.

Back on the subway train, Jake scanned the faces around him. Most avoided his glance and everyone else's, holding their briefcases, shopping bags and purses against their chests or tight in their laps. Some stared out the window of the train at nothing but the blurred lights of the tunnel as they passed. They all looked miserable. The lot of them. Like they'd had the same luck he'd had for the past decade.

A stab of panic shot through Jake. For the past ten years, his meals had been regular. He'd never had to wonder where he would sleep each night. But now that he was free, his next meal was uncertain. He'd gone to the bank earlier and had fifty dollars in his pocket, but how long would that last? Everything, even the cup of coffee he'd bought earlier, seemed to cost a fortune. And a bed…once again, his immediate fate lay in the hands of a woman.

The thought didn't sit well.

It had taken a long time to win his freedom and now that he had it, he was going to make the best of it. He'd applied for three telemarketing jobs this morning. One was sure to pan out. When it did, he'd move out of Shay's apartment.

In the meantime, he had to find a way to appease Shay. He'd thought those intense brown eyes of hers would disintegrate him this morning; they'd been ablaze with anger and disgust. He recalled now that her temper had always been something to contend with, though Jake had never been on the receiving end before.

He pulled a pen and the classified ads from the pocket of the coat and used the half-inch of blank margin space to list the things he would need. This plan had better work or he'd be holding a sign on a street corner somewhere begging for money.

※

Cleopatra Roberts stopped short of putting a maraschino cherry in her mouth. Shay's story had just gotten twice as tantalizing as the piece of fruit dangling between her fingers.

Cleo leaned in closer to sop up all the juice. "Jerome's twin brother just appears in your apartment—out of the blue?"

"Out of *jail*," Shay corrected. "I had no idea he still had a key after all these years."

"But you did know Jerome had a twin?"

"Of course. I grew up with them both." Shay took a sip of her white zinfandel, a little wary of the liquid since her bout with Merlot had ended up griping her stomach in the middle of the night.

"So he shows up, you think it's Jerome surfacing after all these months and you jump his bones?" Cleo said ecstatically.

"Shh!" Shay pushed her hand down to shush her friend.

"I'm so proud of you, girl. It's about time you let out some of those repressed feelings."

"Cleo. You're missing the point," Shay chided her friend. "He took advantage of the situation. He had his tongue in my mouth. His hands were all over me—"

"And you liked it." Cleo grinned and downed her drink. "Tell me I'm lyin'."

"I liked it when I thought it was Jerome, yes. But not now."

"Why? Because this morning, you find him with his weenie in his hand, peeing into a cup?" Cleo was beside herself.

"Yes. It was disgusting. And he had the nerve to excuse the behavior by saying I'd been in the bathroom too long. The man could've knocked on the door. Get real." Shay waved a hand in dismissal.

"Is he just as fine as Jerome?" Cleo asked.

"Cleo," Shay frowned.

"Hey, all I'm saying is you saw more of this brother in two days than you ever did of the one you lived with for ten years. I still can't imagine living with a man so good looking for a decade and never making a move on him." Cleo let her eyes drop to the table. Lost in forbidden thoughts.

Shay shrugged. "We were friends, not lovers."

"Mmm, hmmm." Cleo could see her friend slipping into denial mode. "If it had been me," she started, noting Shay's rolling eyes, "I'd have made Jerome crawl over my near naked body to get out of the door every night—date or no date. That's a fact."

"Forget you, Cleo," Shay said, lifting an eyebrow and smirking at her friend, "you ole two dollah ho."

Cleo sat upright on her barstool and waved a "Vanna-like" hand across the twin missiles she'd just had implanted a few months before. "With these babies, I'm a two *thousand* dollah ho and don't you forget it!"

"You better lower your voice," Shay warned teasingly, taking note of all the male eyes that now peered curiously in their direction. "Someone might take you seriously. Maybe even an undercover cop."

A devilish gleam now shone in Cleo's eyes. "As long as he takes the *undercover* part of his job seriously, I don't see any problem with that."

"Skank," Shay replied, grinning.

"Heifah," Cleo shot back. "You know what you should do?"

Shay flagged down a waiter and ordered another round of drinks. "What?"

"You should take vacation next week and fly out to Vegas with me."

"For that conference you're going to?"

"Yeah. In between sessions, we could gamble, party, take in a show."

"I can't, Cleo." Shay stirred the ice in the empty glass in front of her and wondered what was keeping the waiter with her fresh drink. "You know Cutter creates chaos in my department every time I'm out of the office."

Cleo nodded. "Angelo Cutter hates women."

"Angelo Cutter hates everyone," Shay insisted, grateful for

the drink being placed in front of her. Just thinking about her boss made her angry. She took a greedy gulp of her wine. "But this time, I think he's out to get me."

"What makes you say that?" Cleo frowned.

"He's always in my department, asking my section managers questions he should be asking me about how things are going. It's like he's looking for a problem so he can jump on my case."

"I'm telling you, he's white, you're black...I think the man has issues."

"I would agree with you, Cleo, except he does the same thing to everyone else. Remember John Beaman?"

"Yeah. The guy who used to be the manager of Risk Prevention?"

"Who is now managing three people in a closet in Research," Shay added. "He's as WASP as you can get and you see what Cutter did to him."

"I see your point," Cleo affirmed. "But what are you going to do?"

"I run a clean operation. I'm just hoping he loses interest and moves on."

"To another victim." Cleo twisted her perfect ebony features into a look of pure distaste. "The man's so incompetent,

I can't believe they let him stay around." She reached toward the next barstool to retrieve her coat. "I've got to go, Shay. I'm managing the early shift in the call center tomorrow."

"Okay." Shay hated to see her go. She wasn't ready to face home yet. "I guess I'd better go too."

"Come on," Cleo put a hand on her arm. "The man just cannot be that bad. Once he's done grieving, he'll be fine. Give him a chance. You might learn to like him."

"Too late." Shay shrugged. "I kicked him out. Told him to leave his key and be gone by the time I get home."

She put on her own coat and walked out of the bar with her friend.

"So, are you stalling because you're afraid he didn't listen to you or because he did and you'll go home to an empty apartment?"

"I hate the way you always know what's on my mind, Cleo," Shay said without venom.

"That's what friends are for." Cleo smacked her lips and climbed inside a waiting cab.

Shay waved down the next one lined up on the curb. It was nice to get out of the cold and inside a warm car.

"Where we going?" The cab driver was a woman of about forty with a narrow face and sad eyes. Still, she seemed friendly enough.

Shay gave her address and sat back. As she headed toward home, she tried to decide which of Cleo's scenarios she would be most upset by. She decided it was a dead tie.

Except for her friendship with Cleo, absolutely nothing in Shay's world was right. Everything seemed to be out of control, including Jake, and she hated feeling helpless. "I still have control over who I live with," she said.

"I beg your pardon?" The cab driver's questioning eyes were wide in the rearview mirror.

"Sorry," Shay apologized. "Talking to myself."

The woman nodded her understanding and directed her eyes back to the road.

Shay bit her lip and prayed Jake would be gone when she got home. The last thing she needed was the added burden of comforting him while he grieved for Jerome. Especially since she'd finally gotten her own emotions under control. She really didn't want to deal with a confrontation, but she could if necessary.

Chapter Three

Shay could hear him moving inside the apartment. She took a deep breath, opened the door and stormed her way inside. "Jacob Masters, I thought I told you..." She stopped as the door slammed behind her. The room was dim. Only the reading lamp was on in the living room and it was covered with a red scarf. A single candle sat glowing in the middle of the dining room table. A table set for two.

The room smelled like heaven as the scent of roast beef and baked bread reached her nose. Jake rose from the oversized chair, looking like a movie star dressed in one of Jerome's form-fitting shirts and black slacks.

"Why don't I take this while you kick off those heels and relax?" His voice was deep, thick and as soothing as a long sip of pure Kahlua as he took the collar of her coat in his hands.

The familiar scent of Jerome's cologne now entranced Shay as she accepted Jake's help with her coat. This was exactly like a dream she'd once had. Exactly.

Jake disappeared into her room. Instead of being angry, Shay was spellbound. She held a hand to her grumbling stomach and approached the table. He'd found one of her lace tablecloths and matching white napkins. They looked like elegant swans as they sat in the middle of her good china.

The candle, she noticed, was surrounded by a sea of gorgeous yellow and white carnations that were neatly arranged...in the sipper cup Jake had peed in that morning!

Laughter erupted from Shay as if a dam had broken. She was doubled over when Jake walked back into the room looking extremely pleased with himself.

"I didn't think you'd want to drink out of it again, but I didn't want to throw it out."

"I don't believe you did this," Shay said between bouts of laughter.

"Does that mean you'll forgive me?" he asked seriously.

Shay sobered as she looked into his dark brown eyes. They were so like the man's she once loved. If it were Jerome standing there begging for forgiveness...

"All right, you're forgiven," she said, liking the way his smile deepened his dimples. "But only if your food is as good as your centerpiece," she warned.

"Speaking of which…" Jerome hurried to the kitchen. In moments, he returned with two plates. On each, two thin slices of roast beef covered with rich gravy were neatly displayed, along with potatoes and carrots. Next he brought out warm wheat rolls, butter and a bottle of Merlot, her favorite wine. "I love Merlot," she said, thinking that she should probably pass, given the two glasses of wine she'd had earlier. But it was beginning to feel like a special occasion.

"I noticed," Jake said. "And I appreciate it that you didn't bash me over the head with that empty bottle yesterday." He began to slice his meat as Shay bent her head and folded her hands in prayer.

Blessing a meal. He was a little embarrassed at having forgotten to do so himself. But he was out of practice, it had been so long. He waited until Shay raised her head to take a bite. The meat was tender and succulent and after a couple of bites, Jake couldn't help humming his delight.

"Don't be so pleased with yourself, Jake. I've tasted better," Shay teased.

"I haven't," he said with a mouth full of potatoes. "Not in a very, very long time."

"Was it horrible?" Shay asked. The candlelight made her pale brown skin glow gold and her eyes sparkle. "Is prison as bad as they make out in the movies and on TV?"

Jake could feel himself responding inappropriately to the soft tone of her voice, to the completely feminine way she laid down her fork and sipped her wine. "It is at first," he finally answered. "I fought a lot...until I was left alone."

"You didn't have any friends?"

Jake shook his head. "Not really. Some acquaintances."

"You must've worked out a lot," Shay smiled.

Jake was acutely aware of her eyes as they fell to his arms and chest. "Everyday," he confirmed, feeling another appetite replacing his need for food.

"Thought so. I thought you were going to squeeze me to death yesterday when you grabbed me," she joked, pouring herself another glass of wine.

"I would never hurt you, Shay." He would love another chance to hold her. This time, he would be gentler.

"I know that." She took a long drink of the dark red liquid. "What did you do today other than this?" she asked.

"Well, let's see." Jake cleared his throat and wiped his mouth with his napkin. "I applied for three programming jobs, and two telemarketing positions, just in case. Then I went to visit my mother."

"You did?" Shay seemed delighted. "Was she thrilled to

see you?"

Jake smiled. "Just the opposite. She didn't let me inside the house."

"You're kidding! Are you sure she was home?"

"TV was on. I heard it."

"She must've thought you were a salesman or something," Shay excused.

Jake smiled, "I told her who I was. There couldn't have been a mistake."

Shay swirled the wine in her glass for a moment. "I always wished your mother had been mine, you know?"

Jake nodded. "She used to love it that you called her Mom Two."

"She's a good woman, your mom," Shay frowned. "I can't believe that she'd treat you so badly."

"She's not treating me badly. It's more guilt than anything, I think."

"Guilt?"

"For not believing in me." It was Jake's turn to stare into his glass of wine. "All the evidence was against me. I don't know where all of these supposed eyewitnesses came from, but with every testimony, my story got less and less credible. I didn't have an alibi. I was alone, here in this apartment.

Jerome was out partying somewhere. And I could see it—my mom's faith—leaving her day-by-day. I told her I was innocent and trusted that she knew me well enough to believe me over everything else. Over everyone else.

"But the last thing she said to me before I went to prison was, 'I've never been more ashamed of anyone than I am of you, Jacob. You're no son of mine.'"

"Do you hate her, Jake?" Genuine care shone in her eyes.

"No, but I'm not sure what I feel about her," he admitted. "I just want to talk to her."

"I never wanted to talk to my mother. Not even when she was dying," Shay said bitterly. "I've hated her all my life for making everyday so...so unpredictable. The only thing I could count on was that she would be drunk or high. I never knew if there would be food in the house to eat, if the utilities would be on or off, if strange men would be staying overnight. That's probably the reason I'm so uptight today."

"You're not uptight," Jake chuckled.

"I am," she assured him. "You should look in my closet. Not only do I have all my blouses separated from my slacks and skirts, but I have everything sorted by color. Even my shoes."

"You're just organized," Jake said, suddenly hoping he'd

placed the spices back into the rack in alphabetical order as he'd found them. "There's nothing wrong with organization."

Shay drained her glass and nodded. "That's true. Nothing wrong with organization." She scanned the table before them. "I guess I'd better start on the dishes."

"I'll get them," Jake offered, sensing the Merlot was starting to have an effect on her.

"Really?" She looked at him dreamily. "I don't sleep well if there's a single dirty dish in the house."

"I understand." Jake smiled. "I'll take care of it."

"Okay." Shay sat back in her chair and stretched her arms toward the ceiling as she yawned. "This was a great meal." Her sweater wrapped intimately around soft, round breasts and rose just enough for her belly button to be displayed.

It was decidedly the sexiest thing Jake had ever seen. At least in a long while. He shifted uncomfortably in his chair and tried to look relaxed. "Does that mean I can stay?"

"Sure. But I expect you to find a job and help with expenses."

"That goes without saying," he agreed.

"Okay, then. I'm going to take a hot bath and go to bed. It's been a long day." She pushed away from the table as Jake nearly fell over himself to help her out of her chair.

Shay's hair smelled like perfume. Her eyes were sleepy with wine as she turned to him and smiled. "Thanks, Jake."

"You're more than welcome." Jake felt himself staring at her extraordinary face. Thick, brown spirals of hair fell around a soft, oval face. Though her eyelids drooped with drunken laziness, her eyes were no less brilliant, but seemed more golden than brown now against her pale milk-brown skin. She didn't wear makeup, Jake noted, except a pale shade of lipstick that had almost worn completely off, revealing the palest of pink lips. Jake knew them to be as soft as rose petals and as sweet as nectar. He wanted very much to taste them again.

Before he was tempted further he took a step back. She passed him and headed for the hallway.

"Oh, by the way," Shay had turned around and was standing on unsteadily crossed legs, "Do you need to go potty before I take my bath or were you just going to use our centerpiece?"

"You're evil when you're drunk, you know that?"

"I'm not drunk. But the evil part's accu...accu... right." She laughed and disappeared inside her room.

Blowing out the candle, Jake began clearing dishes from

the table. A promise was a promise and he certainly didn't want to give Shay a reason to kick him out a second time. Besides, he was really starting to like the adult Shay Bennett, bad temper, fiery green eyes and all.

❀

Pain pounded between Shay's temples like a herd of elephants dancing to the shrill beep of her alarm.

Mental note, give up Merlot.

Easing herself out of bed, Shay felt her way down the hall to the bathroom in the dim light. She'd acted silly last night, laughing at a sipper cup full of flowers. And worse, had she really agreed to let Jake stay? Now he would think she was soft and easily manipulated. That was the last thing she wanted the man to believe.

She'd been thinking of Jerome again last night. At one point, she'd imagined it was he sitting opposite her at the table, smiling at her, laughing with her, letting her share her feelings. Maybe that's why she'd let him stay.

Searching the medicine cabinet, Shay found no trace of Tylenol or Motrin. Then she groaned, realizing she'd emptied her last bottle the other night. There was always Midol.

It had to be good for something other than cramps. She slammed back a couple of pills, then reached inside the curtain to turn on the shower.

"Hey, can I get in here first?" Jake was standing in the doorway, a pleading look on his face, his upper torso rippling with muscles.

It took a second for Shay to find her voice. The sight of him in just his jeans weakened her. "Uh…yeah…I still have to get my robe." She turned sideways to let him in and herself out.

"Great. Thanks." Jake hurried to put the seat up. "You can stay and watch if you want, but it's really not all that entertaining."

"Oh. I'm leaving." Shay closed the door quickly and nearly ran to her room. Her heart raced as did her breathing. She held a hand to her chest and tried to quiet the chaos inside. "Wow," she said. Slowly, she sank to the edge of her bed and sat staring at the walls. Her head no longer throbbed, but another, more severe ache had taken its place.

"Finished," he yelled above the background flushing.

Grabbing her robe, Shay gave herself a small slap. "He's just a guy. Get a grip." Determination replaced her need as she headed out of her room and down the hallway with purpose.

Jake was in the kitchen now, banging her cabinets. All the noise was fraying Shay's last nerve. "Do you have to slam the cabinets?" she asked.

"Was I?" he said innocently, sliding a pan onto a front burner. He then pulled a small bowl from another cabinet and a fork from a drawer. He closed one with his foot, the other with his hip before looking up and smiling once more. "Enjoy your shower."

Embarrassed to still be standing in the hallway watching him, fascinated by the way he muscled his way around the kitchen, she bristled. "Stop banging the cabinets. I'll be out in a few minutes."

In exactly thirty-three minutes, Shay managed to shower, get dressed, apply lipstick and pull her curls into a wavy French roll. Jake was now reading the newspaper, drinking coffee, and eating scrambled eggs and bacon.

Looking up from his cup, Jake laid down the paper and beamed his spectacular smile. "You want some breakfast?"

You look like a feast to a starving nation, she wanted to tell him. But she could see how he worked now, manipulating her with sweet smiles, compliments and food. She wasn't falling for it. "I don't eat breakfast."

"I see you're not a morning person." Jake lifted his paper once again. "Sorry I asked."

"I'll be home promptly at six. You are going to continue looking for a job today, right?"

Irritation wrinkled his forehead now as he tossed the paper onto the table. "That's generally why a person would be looking through the classifieds."

"Try the Internet." Shay nodded to the computer desk in the far corner of the room. "You can send a résumé on-line, speed up the process."

"Thanks, I might just do that," Jake gave her an unreadable look, "since we're in such a hurry."

"Good. I'll be home promptly at six."

"Thanks for the warning," he offered just as the door closed behind her.

Shay could tell from his tone that he knew she meant business now. She only hoped work would go as well.

Jake wondered what had gotten into Shay. He thought they'd broken the ice the night before, but this morning she was acting all frosty again. *Why were women so unpredictable?* It was a question that had bothered him all his adulthood.

"Whaddya think, Rome?" He searched the room as if his

brother would materialize. "Should I ask her? Charlotte, I mean," he clarified, clearing his throat. He'd meant the question to be a joke when he asked, but now his gut twisted at the thought of finally confronting the person who'd made his life a living hell. "She knew I wasn't the one." Jake paced the room now, feeling old frustrations build. "But she let me take the fall anyway. And you…" He stopped to look up at the textured ceiling. "No offense, bro, but you lived the fast life all the time and nothing like this ever happened to you. But me…I make the wrong decision one time…"

Jake laughed, dropped his head and shook the thought from his head. "If I know anything now, it's that life *is* ironic. Just when you think you've got it all figured out, it twists around on you."

Jake raised an eyebrow at his next thought. "Which means I should probably let the matter rest between me and Charlotte…but you know that's not going to happen, right?"

Someone—something brushed the back of his head. Jake turned quickly, but saw no one behind him. He studied the window—it was still closed and locked, so what he felt couldn't have been a breeze.

It used to be a signal between him and Jerome. When one said or did something the other disapproved of, the other would palm his head and push it forward playfully.

Allowing his heart rate to settle back into a normal rhythm, Jake sat quietly. Was what he'd felt really his brother's touch? Maybe he just missed him so much that he'd imagined the whole thing.

Jake knew Jerome wouldn't like the idea of his confronting the woman responsible for putting him in jail, he'd said as much the last time they'd been together. But Jake had to know, had to hear from Charlotte's mouth, why she'd accused him falsely. If he could close this one door on his past as soundly as the locks on his old jail cell, Jake felt he could finally be free to move forward into his new life.

Chapter Four

"What exactly do you want from me, Angelo?" Shay crossed her arms and stood firm, ready to battle with her boss. "Everyone makes mistakes. Not that I think this *is* one."

Angelo Cutter's face reddened. Veins popped out on his forehead. "That's the problem with you, Bennett. Your project is falling down around you and you can't even see it." He began pacing the narrow confines of her office.

"We missed one deadline, Angelo. Just one."

"Which pushes our testing, which pushes the launch, which makes for one unhappy client." Angelo held up three fat, shaking fingers. "You and your staff had better find a way to get this e-learning software ready for Team Dynamics on time, or you'll be finding a new job, Bennett. That's all I have to say."

Tears born of frustration stabbed at the backs of Shay's eyes. She pressed them closed, refusing to cry. Angelo was nothing but a bully. A bully who could put her out of a job.

The truth was that she hadn't been paying close attention to the project deadlines lately. She'd been distracted, thinking of Jerome, watching the news, hoping he'd be found. All that had to change, though. And it had to change right now.

Feeling more in control, she circled to the back of her desk and called her assistant. "Mirna, I need to have an emergency meeting with Sydney, Chase and Ray in fifteen minutes."

"Oh. All right, Shay." Mirna sounded half-awake, as usual. "Do you want them in your office?"

"No. Book us a conference room for an hour." It shouldn't take longer than that to give them a good kick in the backsides. "Tell them to be prepared to provide updates on their tasks for the Team Dynamics project."

"Okay. Fifteen minutes, right?"

"Yes," Shay said impatiently. Mirna had been her assistant for a year now, and Shay still hadn't figured her out completely. She talked slow, walked slow, but typed like a Tasmanian devil. "Let me know as soon as you have the room booked."

"Roger," Mirna replied.

Shay hung up abruptly. Why did the woman say goofy things like "Roger?" Was it supposed to be funny? If it was,

Shay didn't get it. Her phone rang. Looking over at the caller ID, she could see it was Cleo. "Hey, girl," she greeted her best friend. "Thought you were on your way to Vegas."

"Just finishing my packing. Do you still have my overnight case? I can't find it."

"I do." Shay put a hand to her forehead. "Sorry. You wanna stop by the apartment and get it?"

"Is the twin hunk still there?" Her tone held a hint of innuendo.

"Yes. I decided to let him stay."

"Really? Why?"

"I'll tell you when you get back. Anyway, you still have a key if he's out, right?"

"Yeah. Thanks. Gotta go."

"Have a good trip. And stay outta them bars, hear?"

"Humph," Cleo replied. "You ain't my mama." Then she added with a laugh. "I'll be good. See ya."

"Bye."

Just as Shay replaced the receiver, the phone rang again. It was Mirna.

"Shay?" she asked as if it could be someone else answering the phone.

"Yes, Mirna."

"You have conference room B from nine-thirty to ten-thirty. I called all of your managers and they'll meet you there." She paused, seemed to catch her breath. "Did you need me to take minutes or anything?"

"Not this time." What she had to say didn't need to be recorded.

Tension arrived along with her managers as Shay sat waiting in the small conference room. Sydney Paradiso was impeccably dressed in a black and white suit, her hair in gleaming black waves molded to the shape of her head. Her makeup was applied so artfully that her chestnut brown complexion appeared flawless. She sat upright, manicured hands folded in front of her on the table. Shay could tell by the look on the woman's face that she was ready to defend against whatever came her way.

Chase Broward was from somewhere in Texas and made sure no one ever forgot it. His hair was the odd brown of a tumbleweed, his skin slightly wrinkled at the eyes. His deep brown eyes shone when he smiled—and he always smiled wider and brighter when he was nervous. Shay noted his grin was a blazing thousand watts this morning.

The last one to enter was Ray Archuleta. This was the manager most likely to blame someone else for whatever went wrong. She hated that about Ray. Shay waited to speak until he adjusted the height of his chair by swirling it in circles and sitting down to pick nervously at his fingernails. She hated that about him, too.

"We missed our deadline to have the e-learning program interface with the scheduling software for Team Dynamics," Shay stated without ceremony. No need to sugarcoat her message. She needed everyone to know how important this was. "I need to know how we can solve this problem without pushing our beta testing out by more than two days."

"I had programmers out sick," Ray started, "and the ones who were here had to meet deadlines on other projects."

Shay narrowed her eyes at the man. "I didn't ask for excuses, Ray. I need solutions and I need them now."

Chase sat up in his chair and cleared his throat. "No offense, Shay," his drawl made him sound as if he had marbles rolling around his tongue, "but I told you more'n a week ago we weren't gonna hit this particular deadline. It's gonna be another week before we can get the specs for the scheduling software. They got some kinda hold up at that vendor."

"Not good enough, Chase," Shay shot back, ignoring the brief stab of guilt. She'd totally disregarded this when he'd mentioned it before. But now wasn't the time to admit to failings. She had to show she was in control. "We've used an interface with the Blue Banana scheduling software for other clients. Why the delay now?"

"Team Dynamics has gone with a totally new version. It's nothing like the old one," Sydney chimed in irritably. "We've been through this before, Shay."

Feeling like a scolded child, Shay could feel her anger mounting. "It hardly matters what we've been through, Syd. Angelo went ballistic in my office this morning. He made it quite clear that if we miss this deadline we'd better have our résumés in order. Now, I for one have no intention of losing my job. If any of you do, please feel free to drop your resignation letters by my office." Pushing to her feet, Shay stormed out of the room before she had the hair-pulling, fist-beating tantrum that was fighting to come out.

Storming into her office, she closed the door for all the solitude she could muster, even though the narrow floor-to-ceiling windows on either side of the door provided little privacy. She turned to her PC and pretended to read her e-mails. The time in the lower corner of the screen read eleven o'clock.

Shay sighed and pulled two pain relievers from the supply in her desk drawer. It was going to be a very long day.

✿

Cleo leapt from the cab and ran toward Shay's apartment. Her plane didn't leave for two-and-a-half hours, but nowadays it took forever to get past the security checkpoint at JFK airport so she needed to get there early. "I'll be back in five minutes," she called back to the driver, an Iranian man with lazy eyes, a turban, and a thick salt and pepper beard.

He grunted something just as the door closed. Cleo took it to be his acknowledgment as she raced up the stairs and through the doors of the red brick complex.

Two steps inside the apartment and Cleo completely forgot why she was there. She was struck dumb by the sight of a magnificent man clothed only in briefs, looking every bit like Jerome Masters as he did pushups. "Oh...hi," she managed.

Jake held his position and looked up at her in surprise. "Hello. Can I help you?"

"In more ways than you can count, I'm sure."

A smile like liquid sunshine spread across his handsome brown face. Deep dimples accented his smile.

Cleo was nearly salivating. Without a doubt he was every

bit as stunning as his brother. Only Jerome had never had muscles quite as large. "I'm Cleopatra—Cleo," she said, taking a step inside the room and closing the door behind her. "And you're—"

"Jake Masters," he said in a low, mellow tone as he rose from the floor.

"I was going to say...*gorgeous*." Cleo nearly purred the last word as her eyes roamed the glistening physique before her. She could pretend to be coy, but it wasn't her style. "I'd love to get further acquainted, Jake, but I'm on my way to the airport." Cleo regretted the necessity to get back to business, but she needed to dump her cosmetics in her case before one of the Ziploc bags she had them in burst open.

"Shay's got my overnight bag. I just need to get it from her room." Cleo rushed to Shay's bedroom.

"Okay," Jake said, returning to his position on the floor. "Looks like you know your way around."

Cleo found the small bag on the top shelf of Shay's closet. She dumped the spare change and nearly empty compacts of eye shadows and blushes onto her friend's bed without ceremony. "Sorry, girl, but I'm in a hurry or I'd clean that up." Swiping a bottle of Red from her friend's dresser, Cleo raced from the room. She'd forgotten to pack her own perfume and knew Shay would understand.

Jake grunted through more pushups as Cleo started across the living room. "Where're you off to, Cleopatra?"

"Vegas. Conference for work," Cleo stated, absolutely loving the way he spoke her full name. "I hope I see you when I get back," she added sincerely. She stopped just short of closing the door. "How many of those do you do?"

Looking up from the floor, Jake panted back an answer. "Dunno. Just keep going until I can't do any more."

"Outstanding." Cleo bit her lip, thinking unclean thoughts about sliding beneath him before remembering she was in a hurry. "Gotta fly. See ya, Jake."

"Bye." Jake liked Shay's friend, though it occurred to him that the two were as opposite as his left and right feet. Shay seemed so self-contained, closed up...except when she was drunk. If he read Cleo correctly, she was fun-loving and flirtatious. Jake loved flirtatious women. They made him feel wanted and needed.

Images of Charlotte flooded his thoughts. Honey-colored skin with dark, sexy brown eyes. Lips the color of raspberries. He had just been doing her a favor, escorting her home that night. She'd looked so helpless when she'd asked him in her throaty voice thickened with liquor. She'd been so grateful and complimentary when he'd walked her to her door. She'd thanked him with soft kisses and before he knew it, he was sitting on her leather couch, straddled by her strong soft thighs, feasting on her lush breasts.

Jake had had no intention of sleeping with her when he'd driven her home. She'd bewitched him somehow. He frowned and lowered himself on exhausted arms to the floor. That one hour, that one seemingly innocuous act of sex, had changed his life forever.

"Damn her." He laid his head on his hands and enjoyed the cool hardwood floor under his hot body. "I just want to know why."

A loud, guttural noise brought Charlotte to the edge of consciousness. She attempted to roll over, but a weight draped her body, preventing movement.

Best she didn't move anyhow.   Her head hurt.

She brought a hand up to her throbbing temple. A bass heavy rhythm pounded in her head like Damian's souped-up car stereo.

Damian. She hoped he was wondering where she was.

The guttural noise started again. Snoring.

Charlotte shoved at the man lying across her breasts. "Smokey." Her voice was hoarse.

Smokey didn't budge.

She opened her eyes cautiously. Viciously bright slivers of light assaulted her mascara-coated eyes, forcing her to cover her face.

Groggy thoughts and dim visions of last night's party played in her brain as she smacked against the nasty remnants of the six Fuzzy Navels and four Amaretto Sours coating her tongue.

Charlotte smiled and stretched beneath Smokey's dead weight. A good party. A good lay. She'd needed it after the grilling Damian had given her yesterday.

How many times had he asked her, "What did you do with the money? What did you buy?" He'd acted like she was supposed to be dependent upon him for everything. She'd be damned if she'd beg for money if she wanted it. They had plenty.

"Good old Smokey don't ask questions. He knows how to have a good time. Huh, Smokey?" She shoved at the lump of dark flesh again.

"Wha—?" He lifted a heavy eyelid. "You say somethin'?"

His breath was foul and his heavy body was starting to make her sweat. "I gotta go. Let me up."

"Oh. Sure, sweet thang." He leered briefly before rolling off her and going back to sleep.

She waded through the clothes and empty alcohol bottles on Smokey's floor into the bathroom. She swiped a wet washcloth with soap and cleaned her armpits and between her legs. The important parts.

Carefully, she splashed water on her face. A long look in the mirror confirmed that she looked as tired as she felt.

She pulled foundation from her purse and concealed the dark circles under her eyes as best she could. A few moments later, satisfied that she'd successfully camouflaged the ill effects of her late evening, she returned to the bedroom. But the hurt inside was becoming a lot harder to conceal.

She pulled on a loose sweater, long skirt and flat shoes and pulled her shoulder length brown hair into a ponytail before heading for the door. It was time to get home. She sighed heavily, wishing she were going anywhere but there.

The drive to her four-thousand-square-foot home was unmercilessly brief. In only a half-hour she was standing in the spacious living room with vaulted ceilings and tiled floors, feeling sick to her stomach.

She loathed this place. Hated the smell of pine cleaner her housekeeper used. Hated the antique furniture and expensive Persian rugs. Hated the kitchen with its rows of shiny copper cookware hanging from the ceiling rack. But what she hated most was how empty she felt in the house. She'd decorated the thing at least a dozen times trying to make it feel comfortable. Make it feel...like home.

Dropping her purse and keys next to the couch, Charlotte made her way to the kitchen. She was hungry. At least there was something she could do about that.

Damian stood at the bay window near the breakfast table, staring at the lush gardens of their backyard.

Instantly, a chill shimmied up Charlotte's back. Why was he here? He should've been at work by now. Instead, he was in his robe, black stubble on his teak brown face, drinking a cup of coffee. He nearly dropped his cup on the table as he turned at her entrance. "Where've you been?"

Charlotte didn't like the wild, panicked look around his eyes. "You know where I've been." She reached inside her bag for the roll of money she'd tucked away the night before. "It's all there," she said quietly, knowing he'd count it anyway.

"Tell your sister she can't borrow any more money," he

said, flipping through the bills. Once he was satisfied that the entire twenty-five hundred was there, he tucked it into his robe pocket and put a hand to Charlotte's face. "Where were you last night? Did you stay at your sister's house?"

For a moment, Charlotte thought of telling him the truth, but decided to make him work it out of her. "No. We had a fight," she explained, pulling away from him to get to the refrigerator.

"Oh. That would explain why she said you weren't there when I called. 'Course she said she hadn't seen you at all yesterday." His tone was heavy with accusation.

Feigning impatience, Charlotte pulled two eggs and bacon from the refrigerator and scolded her husband. "Does that surprise you? I told you, we had a fight. Cherese always tries to get me in trouble when she's mad at me. I stayed in the LaQuinta off the interchange last night." Knowing this would probably settle the matter, she went about preparing her breakfast.

"You must think I have the IQ of a child," Damian said in a low, calm voice. He never yelled. When he was upset his voice dropped to a near whisper, as it did now. "I think the least I deserve is the truth."

Now wasn't the time for the truth, she decided. She wasn't ready. Breaking their pact of ten years might be the one thing capable of shattering Damian's glacier-cool demeanor and Charlotte wanted to make sure she had a safe harbor when the ice cracked. "I just needed a night out, Damian. I went to a party at a friend's house and fell asleep."

"Why didn't you tell me before you went?" he asked. His eyes were dark with distrust.

Charlotte shrugged. "I'm not like you, Damian, I can't plan every activity. It was a spur of the moment invite, so I made a spur of the moment decision. I didn't leave until ten. You were still at work," she added.

Predictably, Damian retreated from his attack. "We were preparing closing arguments on the Treadwell case. I—"

Charlotte held up a palm to stop him mid-explanation. "It's okay. I just can't sit at home all the time. I feel smothered." *Like now.* "Like I don't have any freedom to do what I want without your permission." She softened her eyes and moved her lips to her husband's. "Sometimes I just need to be able to go out somewhere fun. On a whim. Whenever I please."

"You are free to do what you want, Charlotte," Damian's voice lost its edge, "but I want you to be here more than you're somewhere else. I want you to be with me." He moved to take her into a suffocating embrace.

How did she tell him that he was the last person she wanted to be with? "I'm here," she managed a seductive smile, "with you." For a little while longer, she decided.

Charlotte pushed her hands through the opening in his robe and massaged him slowly. It took only a second for him to respond.

"Damn you, woman," his voice was ragged as he laid back his head and allowed her the freedom to trail kisses down his stomach. He knew Charlotte was just avoiding a serious conversation about where she really was last night, but he found it hard to care. "Ohhhh," he sighed as she sent heavenly sensations throughout his body.

Grasping her shoulders, he held on tight, his feet losing touch with the ground. Floating on the ecstasy of lust, of desire, he cried out his wife's name over and over until finally, his love spilled into her hands.

She left him panting to wash her hands in the sink. Goose flesh rose on the back of her neck as he came up behind her. His breath smelled of old liquor laced with coffee. "Do you know how much I love you, Charlotte?" His whisper held a hint of panic.

"I know, baby." Charlotte's gut tightened with guilt. She dried her hands on a paper towel and fought the impulse to pull away. "I'm tired, Damian," she said. "And you should be at work."

"I told my partner to handle the closing argument. I took the day off." He offered a lusty laugh. "That means we can take a nap together." He pulled up her skirt and began massaging her bottom. "And later," he kissed her neck and circled his hands to her breasts, "I'll treat you to a nice lunch. Doesn't that sound like fun?"

"Yeah. It sounds great," Charlotte said, trying to discern where she'd find the energy to keep up her loving wife charade for the rest of the day. She followed him to the bedroom. As he dropped his robe and climbed into their unmade bed, she headed for the bathroom. "Try to find your second wind, baby. I'll be back in a minute."

"Already found it," he said with a hearty pelvic thrust.

Charlotte saw that, unfortunately, he had. "Hold that thought," she teased. It was a relief to close the door and have a moment just to breathe without him being in the same space. Quietly, she turned the lock on the bathroom door, not wanting to risk his intrusion.

Sighing, Charlotte dropped heavily onto the stool in front of her vanity. She stared at the large marquis diamond on her left hand for a moment. "You've gotta find a way out of this, girl," she said to herself.

Shifting her attention to her right hand, she stared at the gorgeous jade ring she'd bought from one of her friends at the club. It was her favorite ring. Twisting the opaque green jewel away from the ring's base was like peeling the wrap from a Christmas present. Sitting as pure as snow in the stainless steel orifice was a glorious white powder. And she liked this stuff too much to give it up, though Damian hated that she used it.

That's why he was always so interested in how much money she had. He didn't want her buying drugs. He thought because he had all the money, he could call all the shots.

Just like her father, just like Machete, her ex-pimp.

Charlotte tapped about half of the cocaine onto her marble countertop, then carefully closed the ring to its original position.

"Maybe I'll cut him off from sex," she murmured. "I'll have sex with everyone but him. That ought to make him mad enough to divorce me." She then took two huge sniffs. When the drugs hit her brain, the plan sounded ingenious. Why fight to get out of your cell when you could get the guard to open the door and set you free?

Euphoria helped her to her feet. Charlotte checked herself in the mirror and dusted the remaining powder from her nose. She opened the door and prepared to put her perfect plan into action. *Or inaction,* she thought with a giggle.

Chapter Five

It felt as if a knife were lodged between Shay's shoulder blades. She'd been working the Team Dynamics problem all day, calling on her contacts at Blue Banana to obtain the specs for their new application and planting the seeds for future product collaboration, then pushing her managers to get the programming in place to solve the integration issue.

A tense and tired group of managers were now assembled in her office. "Okay, give it to me straight," she stated. "Where're we now?"

Chase was the first to answer. "I think we've got it solved." His dark eyes held a spark of enthusiasm. "Still needs to be tested, but we're optimistic."

"How optimistic?" Shay pushed. "It's important that this is ready to go by tomorrow."

"It's seven o'clock, Shay." It was Sydney who spoke. "We can test first thing in the morning." She put her hands up quickly as Shay started to speak. "They'll be here early, I promise."

"Fine." Shay would've liked to tell Angelo that they had completely resolved the problem, but she knew unexpected things could happen during testing to take them two steps backward. "When will we know for sure if this fix works?"

Sydney shrugged and looked toward Ray for assistance in answering the question. "With your folks testing along with mine, we should know by...what? Noon?"

"About," Ray agreed. His ever-trembling fingers pushed through his black waves wearily. "Unless something blows up on us."

This last comment earned him a stinging glare from Chase. "Nothing's gonna blow up. Checked the code myself," he assured his co-worker.

Ray backed further against the office wall, palms up in defense. "No offense, man."

Just as quickly, Chase let go of his irritation and sat back in his chair. "Gotta hand it to ya, boss," he said with his crooked grin. "You bulldozed some major roadblocks for us today. I, for one, 'preciate the assist."

Sydney and Ray also chimed in with grudging thanks for what she'd done.

Shay stood up and reached for her coat and purse. "No need to thank me. But I want to point out that you all had the opportunity to push past these things yourselves. I expect more initiative in the future." She threw on her coat and grabbed her scarf from the hook on the door. "I'll see you all bright and early tomorrow."

Shay headed for the elevators, grateful that the day had finally ended. She was going home and taking a long, hot bath—with bubbles. Closing her eyes, she imagined how wonderful the hot water was going to feel. Maybe she'd light some scented candles and have a glass of wine.

The elevator *dinged* on the ninth floor and Shay suddenly remembered that she'd left her purse in her office. She'd set it down when she'd put on her coat and had forgotten to take it with her in her haste. "Dang it." Her irritation caused a fresh stab of pain between her shoulder blades.

When the doors opened, Shay pushed past the janitor and her cleaning cart, then stabbed at the up button on the wall. It didn't take long for the other elevator to arrive and she rode it back to the fifteenth floor. As she rounded the corner to her office, it surprised her to see the light still on. The least one of them could've done was turn it off. A few feet from the door, she heard voices.

"Damn, man. You tried to compliment her and all she could do was turn it around on us. Like we could've done what she did today." It was Ray complaining.

"If she'd shown any interest at all in the project before now, we wouldn't be behind," Sydney added. "We needed her to throw her weight around long before this."

"Now, it ain't like she's a bad manager—"

"I didn't say she was a bad manager," Sydney cut off Chase. "She's smart, knows how to solve problems, but she's mean as a viper. I'm this close to quitting. I'm fifty years old. I don't appreciate being treated like a child by a thirty-year-old."

The comments stung. Shay wanted to turn tail and run the other way. But then what? Hide out in the women's room until they all finally left?

"I know what she needs." Chase's drawl grew more pronounced. "A good roll in the hay'd take all the mean out of that viper."

"Oh, for heaven's sake." Shay could almost see Sydney rolling her eyes at that comment. "You men think sex'll solve everything, don't you?"

"Yeah," both men said in unison.

Hearing them move around as they laughed, Shay shrugged back hurt feelings.

"There's no hope of her getting any, though," Ray added.

"She's all about business all the time."

"Maybe she doesn't like men," Chase offered.

"Now you guys are going off the deep end," Sydney said, "although I have to admit, she's very aggressive."

Shay couldn't believe what they were saying. She was a senior manager. She was supposed to be professional and what did it didn't matter if she was heterosexual or homosexual? Her life wasn't any of their damned business. It was time she interrupted their Shay-bashing party. Taking a deep breath, she strode into the office with purpose.

The laughter was shut off as quickly as a running faucet.

"What are you all still doing here?" Shay asked in mock surprise. "I'd thought you'd be halfway home by now."

Chase hemmed and hawed a bit before answering. "We were on our way. Just clampin' down on some loose ends."

Right. Reaching for her bag, Shay avoided all eye contact, knowing she wouldn't be able to hide the hurt. "I forgot my purse," she said quickly. "Don't forget to turn off the lights when you leave," she added before escaping the heavy layers of discomfort crowding her office.

"Do you think she overheard us?" Sydney's whisper was all Shay heard as she raced down the hallway for the second time that evening.

❉

The door slammed. Jake looked up from his simmering pot of spaghetti sauce in time to see Shay removing her coat and whipping it around to drape on her arm like a bullfighter's cape. He glimpsed eyes red-rimmed with exhaustion and thought better of the cheerful greeting he was about to offer. "Rough day?" he asked instead.

"I'd rather not talk about it," she said crisply before disappearing down hallway into her bedroom. She slammed that door, too.

Jake could see it would be in his own self-interest to stay away from her tonight. Of course, if Shay didn't come out of her room for the rest of the evening, he'd have the television to himself. It was hard work looking for a job…and not getting one. He'd had two interviews today for programmer jobs, but they all wanted experience in programming languages he'd never heard of. "C++" used to mean you almost had a "B" in math. And Java? Java was coffee last he'd heard.

Turning the burner off below his sauce, Jake prepared himself a heaping plate of spaghetti, covered it in sauce and sprinkled Parmesan on top. His mouth was salivating by the time he reached the table. Swinging a chair over to rest his foot on, he retrieved the remote and turned the television to ESPN, hoping to find a good basketball game.

Satisfied to watch the Tennessee Lady Vols and South Carolina State University's women's team in tight contention, Jake settled into his meal.

Clothed in her thick robe, Shay chose that moment to storm out of her room and into the kitchen. She pulled the refrigerator door open with such force Jake could hear glass clinking.

"What happened to the rest of that Merlot?" she asked, her head still buried in the fridge, her rear end extended just past the open door.

"Bottom shelf," Jake shot over his shoulder at her, then turned back to his spaghetti. "Startin' to make drinking that stuff kind of a habit, aren't you?"

"I wasn't asking permission," she shot back, bottle in hand. She opened a cabinet and retrieved a wine glass and stormed into the bathroom. A moment later, Jake could hear bath water running.

"Just an observation," he said quietly, studying the closed door. Jake could tell something had happened to her today. But he doubted she'd ever admit it. Damned woman seemed hell-bent on taking on everything alone. Of course, he reasoned, her best friend was out of town so she didn't have much choice.

"Well, Jake," he rose from the table, "looks like it's in your hands." He felt a comforting pressure on his shoulder. "Jerome?" Turning to look behind him, Jake was disappointed to see only the wall and a ficus tree standing where his brother should've been.

"This is getting weird." Jake wondered briefly about his sanity before moving on to the task at hand. He walked over to study the couch cushions. Deciding they would serve his purpose nicely, he moved the coffee table to the side and pulled the cushions onto the floor. He then retrieved a bottle of Super Six Oil and a bed sheet from his room. After spreading the sheet over the cushion, he turned off the ceiling light.

Shay had scented candles by the dozens in one of the kitchen cabinets. Jake arranged them on the coffee table and lit them. He was standing, admiring the soothing effect of the great-smelling candlelit room when Shay emerged from the bathroom.

"What are you doing?" Shay asked, entering the living room. "Those are my candles."

"I know. I lit them for you." Jake smiled and took her

hand. "I noticed you looked a little stressed when you came home this evening and thought I might be able to help."

"By doing what?" Reluctantly she allowed herself to be led to the sheet-covered couch cushions lying on the floor.

"Lie down," Jake instructed.

"I'm not in the mood—"

"Lie down," Jake insisted. "On your stomach."

"Look, Jake." Shay turned on him. "I don't like you in that way, okay?"

"When I get done with this massage, you still won't like me. You'll love me."

His grin was so smug, she was inclined to believe him. "Massage?"

"Yeah." He nodded. "If you lie down," he added sternly.

Even after the hot bath and a half bottle of wine, Shay's shoulders ached as if they were on fire. Maybe a massage would help. "All right." Shay eased herself down on the cushions.

"You'll need to open that robe, or I won't be able to do this," Jake said.

"Oh." Clumsily, Shay came up to her knees, untied the belt, laid down back down, and then slid the robe out from beneath her. "All right, I'm ready," she said a little breathlessly, feeling a bit slutty for actually wanting the man to touch her body once again.

First the cool air of the room touched her back as he slid the robe down to the rise of her hips. Vulnerability and discomfort created a small panic in Shay's belly. "You know, Jake—" She set her hands on the floor to push herself up, but before she could get the words out to tell him she'd changed her mind, a trail of warm oil hit her back and was immediately followed by the solid pressure of Jake's hands.

It shocked Shay at first, it had been so long since she'd felt a man's touch on her body. It felt wrong. It felt nice. Jake took her hands and gently moved them so that her arms were straight alongside her back. He kneeled near her head then and began pushing his hands from her shoulders to her hips in long, fluid strokes. The feel of his fingers fanning the top of her hips before trailing back up again was soothing, relaxing, and, unfortunately, far too sensuous. His warm, strong hands were slowly stirring up needs within her she'd rather have kept stored and locked away.

Jake moved behind her, straddling her bottom between the solid muscles of his thighs. If Shay hadn't been lying down, she would have fallen from the sudden heat that rushed from her pelvis to her head. The desire that had been on a slow simmer began to boil as his skillful hands went back to work. Jake kneaded the fiery knot between her shoulders, slid up the back of her neck and down again to follow the flow of her shoulders. A moan of pleasure slipped past her lips before she could stop it.

To his credit, Jake didn't acknowledge that he'd heard it. He just kept repeating the soothing movement to her neck and shoulders, easing the fire between her shoulder blades, easing the tension in her mind. Equally, he relaxed and excited her with his careful strokes that now flowed down the length of her spine back to her hips. More warm oil hit her back and his strokes deepened and slowed as he traveled the outsides of her back to her shoulders, then slowly traveled down her arms to her hands. When Jake laced his warm, slick fingers between hers and pushed back gently and held her hand in a slight stretch, Shay lost all touch with reality.

She realized it was part of the massage but couldn't help reacting to the intimacy of their hands being joined. She hadn't been close to anyone for such a long time, and certainly not to anyone who had thought to give her a massage simply because she was tense.

For the third time that day, tears threatened, but this time,

Shay was tempted just to let them flow. After all, if anyone would understand her feelings, she felt it would be Jake.

"What happened today?" Jake asked quietly, as if sensing now was the time to speak. "You're as tense as a tightrope."

"You don't want to know." Shay swallowed hard against the thickness in her throat and kept her eyes shut so as not to betray her feelings. She wasn't ready to trust him yet.

"I wouldn't ask if I didn't want to know."

"Jerome never asked," she offered. "It was always me listening to his problems. I didn't mind, though."

"Oh yeah? What kind of problems? I didn't think my brother had any."

"Women problems," Shay offered with a chuckle. Jerome was a safe enough subject. "He never could figure out how to make a relationship last longer than a couple of months."

"Yeah. I got the impression there were a few women in his life. A new name came up every time he visited me. "So, you and Jerome never...?"

It was a sore subject, but Shay tried to sound nonchalant. "No. Even if I had wanted to...anyway, I knew what I'd be in for, so I never tried. It would've complicated our living arrangement."

"You had feelings for him, though." It was more statement

than question.

Shay said nothing, simply shrugged.

"Did you love him?" Jake asked so quietly she wondered if it was simply an echo of her own thoughts.

"I thought so," she admitted just as quietly.

His hands never stopped. They continued their soothing strokes up her back, and slowly, heavenly, back down to her hips.

"I always wondered why he never even thought about me in that way," Shay said, appalled at hearing her thoughts being spoken out loud. Yet she couldn't stop them. "What was so wrong with me?" There it was. Her heart was sitting out on her sleeve in full view now. Dear God, why had she let that slip? Jake had no business knowing this much about her.

"Wanna know what I think?" Jake brought her robe back up to cover her shoulders, then moved the bottom of her robe aside to uncover one butt cheek and her right leg. He tucked the remaining material lightly between her legs.

Shay tensed, uncertain of what Jake was doing now…and what he would say if she acknowledged his question. Warm oil fell in heavenly drops onto her bottom, down her thighs, to her calf. Relaxing once again, she asked, "What do you think?"

"I think there's nothing wrong with you. I think there's so much that's right that Jerome didn't think he was worthy."

The heel of Jake's hands kneaded her bottom in a slow, steady, circular motion. Shay was surprised by Jake's answer...and completely touched.

No words could describe the feelings swirling around Shay's gut, her head, her heart. Gratitude, comfort, and desire mixed in equal measure began a slow boil in her veins. A full body flush heated Shay from head to toe, fueled by the sensation of Jake's hands palming her thigh, one moving inside the thigh, then out, and the other hand moving inside, then out. He made his way deliberately down her leg to her feet. Again she sighed audibly as the man soothed away the effects of eleven hours in high heels with his wonderfully gifted hands.

Covering her right side, Jake gave identical treatment to the left. By the time he'd reached her other thigh with his push me, pull you move, Shay was in full-blown heat. Desire had her pressing her pelvis deep into the cushions below her.

There was no delicate way to admit it. She wanted Jake in the worst way. Well...maybe not Jake. What she really wanted was to pretend it was Jerome touching her, making her body sing like a Toni Braxton ballad. All she wanted was to feel, just once, what it would've been like to make love to him. Maybe Jake wouldn't mind. If she told him how much she needed to feel him inside her right now. All she had to do was roll over and—. *Forget it, Shay.*

"How're you feeling now?" Jake asked. His hands trembled as he covered her once again with her robe. This wasn't where he usually ended his massages, but decided it would be best if he stopped now. His relationship with Shay was hanging by a thread at best. Now was not the time to blow it by doing something stupid.

Shay rolled onto her side and her robe fell discreetly to cover the parts of her body Jake still wanted badly to touch. "Honestly?" she asked.

Jake noted how dark her green eyes were as she looked at him. The erection he'd carried since he first touched her silken skin now nearly launched itself out of his pants with hopefulness.

It had been a long time since Jake had had any dealings with the fairer sex, but he knew lust when he saw it. His heart bounced around like a child's toy ball in his chest. "Honesty is always the best policy," he said, hoping desperately for her to open that robe and let him in.

"I'm hungry." With that, she rose from the cushions, tying her belt firmly around her.

Jake heard steel bars closing soundly on his hope for sex. A thousand curses went flying through his brain.

"Any more of that spaghetti left?" She headed for the kitchen.

"Yeah." Jake looked at his hands, rubbing the remaining oil into his palms with the force he wished he could apply elsewhere. "Plenty. I need to, uh, go wash my hands."

Jake went to the bathroom and closed the door. He turned on the faucet and splashed cold water on his face before sitting down heavily on the toilet seat. "Idiot," he scolded himself soundly. Had he really expected her to fall under his spell simply because he'd given her a massage?

It had worked before with other women. But Shay wasn't just another woman. He'd meant it when he'd told her what he thought about Jerome's feelings toward her. How else could he explain his brother not even mentioning the fact he was living with her? Jerome told him everything. Why not this?

"You *did* love her, didn't you, bro?" he asked the air. There was no pressure on his head or shoulder, real or imagined. This time Jake hadn't expected there to be. A new question now hung in the air, though. A question for Jake.

He gave only a moment's thought to it, not quite sure of the truth yet. "I don't know if I'm in love with her either, Rome," Jake smiled at his next thought, "but I sure wanted her bad just a few minutes ago."

Sobering, he dried his face on a hanging towel, careful to place it back on the rack. He turned off the water he'd let run and stared at himself in the mirror for a moment. "Think with your brain, man. Your brain," he said insistently.

Feeling more in control, he left the bathroom. Shay was at the table attacking her plate of spaghetti as if she'd never seen food before. "How is it?" he asked, replacing the cushions on the couch.

"Good," she said. "I don't think I ate all day."

"You don't remember?"

"I was busy."

Jake sat opposite her at the table. "Problems?"

Shay shrugged. "Nothing I couldn't handle."

Narrowing his eyes, Jake tried to assess the likelihood of having his next question answered. Fifty-fifty, he guessed. "Then what had you so upset?"

Her green eyes penetrated him to the bone. "Listen, Jake. I'm trying to stay out of your business, I would appreciate it if you stayed out of mine."

Jake sighed and leaned back in his chair. "All right. Just trying to be a good roommate."

"A good roommate would have a job by now so he could help pay the rent," she bristled.

Jake smiled. "I'm accepting a position as a telemarketer tomorrow. I was trying to hold out for a programming job, but it looks like my skills have gone the way of the dinosaur."

Surprise knocked some of the heat from her eyes. "Oh. Good."

"It doesn't pay all that well, but it's something."

"Okay. Let me know when you get paid and we'll start dividing up the bills." Shay rose to take her plate to the kitchen.

"I'll get the dishes," Jake offered.

Another heated glare from across the kitchen counter. "I did manage to keep my apartment in order prior to your coming. I *can* handle the dishes."

"Fine. Do the dishes." Jake rose and decided to find something else to watch on television. He was growing weary of trying to break the ice with Shay.

A half-hour later, he was flipping the channel between two NBA games when he noticed Shay standing nearby. Jake glanced up to see if she wanted something. She had an odd look on her face.

"I'm sorry," she said simply. "I've been rude and abrupt"

"It's okay," Jake excused.

"No. It's not." Shay sat down next to him on the edge of the couch. "I guess I've been the same way at work and...I overheard my staff saying something to that effect tonight. It upset me." Her fingers trembled as she pulled at each nail in turn.

Her hands were delicate things. Long fingers with unpolished nails all filed to the same no-nonsense length. Jake put an arm around her shoulders and pulled her into his arms. He said nothing, sensing that more words would only make this difficult for her.

It took a moment for her to relax and lean on him. Jake stroked the cottony spirals of her hair that smelled like flowers. She was warm and soft and felt absolutely perfect in his arms. He laid a cheek on her hair and smiled. Maybe the ice was broken after all.

Chapter Six

"Jacob, my man, I think you just fell down the damned rabbit hole." Jake scanned the large room. Row after row of gray cubicles filled the space like a giant mouse maze. It was unexpectedly quiet, given the number of T-shirt and blue jean-clad employees all talking at once into their head-sets.

A heavy hand fell on Jake's shoulder. "Not quite what you'd expected, huh?" Lela Perez was the manager of the Quantum Call Center. She was as tall as Jake, had to weigh a full three hundred pounds, had short, spiky blond-gray hair and had more tattoos on her arms and neck than the entire prison population of the state penitentiary.

"Not quite," Jake said, suddenly feeling way overdressed in his pressed slacks and dress shirt. "Is there anyone here over age nineteen besides you and me?" Suddenly, his thirty-six years felt ancient. He guessed his new boss to be around forty-five.

"Most folks don't like working the night shift. Got a lot of insomniacs calling in to order from the infomercials in the middle of the night, but they all got money from their day jobs. The kids do it for the money, but they turn over so fast, I can't keep their names straight. That's why I latched on to you, Jake." She gave his back an hearty slap. "An ex-inmate. How many options have *you* got?" She exploded into boisterous laughter. "No offense," she added.

"None taken." Jake followed her down an aisle of the maze. She stopped in front of a box half the size of his old prison cell and waved an arm ceremoniously over the low walls.

"This is it. Your home away from home. Time to put that four hours of training to work. Got your scripts?"

Jake raised the thin binder confidently.

"Great." Lela checked her watch. "Your section manager is Nicole Grundhoeffer. She should've been here by now, but if you run into any trouble," she turned to the cube behind her, "just ask Donald Petit-Pool here."

The name sounded like *Petty Pool* to Jake.

Lela continued, "His last name is French for 'little chicken.' We just call him Sing-Sing since that's what he does between calls." The young man smiled, making his blue eyes sparkle. He nodded his acknowledgment but continued talking into his headset and typing in the order the customer was placing.

"Sing-Sing! Ha!" Lela suddenly realized what the words could mean to Jake. "Like the prison. Get it, Jake?"

"I get it." Jake smiled as he took his seat inside the tiny cube as the aging biker chick headed back toward her office. "I should've asked for more money," he said to himself.

"Think bonus." Donald stood up in his cube and pulled his headset down around his neck. He was clean cut, blond and looked like every white schoolgirl's dream. Probably a college boy, Jake guessed. "The real money's in the bonuses they pay."

"That good, huh?" Jake asked, now interested.

"I made enough in my first three months to put a down payment on a new Ford F150 dark blue truck with sterling silver rims. The girls at the community college cream over it."

"They ain't the only ones, baby." This from the man opposite the aisle from Jake. He was short, had neatly trimmed dark hair with brown highlights and the even brown coloring of a Latino. The name on the cube was Oscar Aguirre. The man was so pretty he could have been Prince.

Oscar turned to Jake, then walked the short distance across the aisle and offered a hand. "You ain't so bad either, Mr...?"

"Masters. Jake Masters." Jake shook his hand, paying special note to the welcome in the man's dark brown eyes. He'd seen the look before—many times. It had stopped freaking him out years ago, though. Now Jake accepted it as a compliment. "Nice to meet you, Oscar."

"Hetero?" Oscar asked about his sexual preference.

Jake nodded. "But if that changes at any time, you'll be the first to know."

A grin as wide as Broadway beamed on Oscar's face. "I'd be glad to be your slave, Mr. Masters."

"Oh, Oscar." Donald put a hand to his heart. "You'd just kick me to the curb like that?"

"Ah, don't get upset, Sing-Sing. There's room in my heart for you both."

Deciding this new job would be anything but dull, Jake took a look at his equipment. A headset, a PC and a phone that had double-digit numbers blinking across the caller ID screen. "Don't these numbers mean we have calls waiting?" Jake asked his new friends.

"Yes, it does." Donald rubbed his hands together. "Dollar bills, man. Dollar bills." He was back in his seat with his headset on before Jake could blink.

Oscar moved with much less enthusiasm back to his cube.

"Where the hell is Nicole?" he asked, checking his watch. "I'm due for a break. If she ain't here in five minutes, I'm goin' anyway."

Since he didn't appear to be expecting an answer, Jake donned his own headset and pulled out his help scripts. He punched in his ID number and took a deep breath before hitting the on screen button to put him on duty. "Here goes nothing," he said, then clicked the *On* button on his PC screen.

About four hours into his session, Jake realized that he seemed to get much better results cross-selling the "extras" they were supposed to offer to the women callers rather than the men. They responded much more favorably to his friendly chit-chat and seemed to buy because of the time he took with them.

The past five callers had been men who'd only purchased what they'd called in for. The bonuses were in the cross-sells though, so Jake was thrilled when his next caller was a woman.

"Thank you for calling the Ab-mania customer service line. May I have your name?" Jake asked, according to script. He placed his fingers gingerly over his keyboard, ready to type in the woman's information.

"Charlotte White," she answered.

Jake froze. He didn't breathe, think, move or have a heartbeat for a full five seconds.

"Hello?" the woman voice queried. "Are you still there?"

"Yes." The initial shock of hearing her voice again wore off, leaving a strange tingling in his spine. "Yes, uh, sorry about that. Your name is Charlotte White. May I have your telephone number, area code first?"

Sitting up straight in his chair, Jake grew excited. It was like a gift from God or something. Here was the woman who'd placed him in jail about to give him her phone number and address. It was like Fate.

Carefully Jake typed in the telephone number, then her address, repeating it all to commit it to memory. She was living in New Jersey. Not far.

"And how many sets of Ab-mania videos would you like to order, Ms. White?"

"Oh. Just one."

"From the sound of your voice, I'd be surprised if you even needed these tapes," he teased, knowing if she looked anything like she did ten years ago, her figure didn't need any help at all.

"How sweet," she said with a seductive laugh. "But it's not

for me. It's for my sister. She had her last child five years ago, but she still looks like she's eight months pregnant."

Ouch. "I can tell you love your sister dearly," Jake teased. "Would you like to include a full year's subscription to *Fitness Magazine* as well? It's half off the normal subscription price tonight."

"Tempting...but I think I'll do enough damage with just the tape. It's her thirty-fifth birthday. Her husband's giving her a surprise party. He wanted some gag gifts and some real ones. Sweet, huh?" There was a hint of sadness or envy or something in her voice.

"Very sweet," Jake acknowledged.

"You know...what's your name?" Charlotte asked.

"Oscar," Jake offered quickly, glancing at the real Oscar, hoping he hadn't overheard.

"You know, Oscar. Your voice reminds me of someone I once knew."

"Really?" Jake wondered if she remembered his voice after all this time.

"Um, hm." She was silent for a moment. "He was a nice guy."

She couldn't be talking about him, he thought irritably. You don't put nice guys in prison. "The total for your order is $59.95. Did you want to put this on your credit card?

"What kind do you take?"

"The usual. MasterCard, American Express, Visa."

"Let's do Visa," she said. A man's voice called out in the background.

Jake couldn't hear what the man was saying, but he heard Charlotte's muffled reply. "I couldn't sleep. No. Just go back to bed, Damian." It was a much more agitated Charlotte White that now spoke to Jake. "Sorry about that. Let me give you the credit card number real quick. I gotta go."

"Go ahead." Jake typed in the number dutifully. "Thank you, Mrs. White. You have a good evening."

According to the schedule, it was time for Jake to have a break. He needed it. The conversation with Charlotte had brought back bad feelings. Not to mention his butt was molding to the shape of the chair and his bladder was fuller than his stomach. He placed himself on *Break* on the computer and tried to remember the direction to the restrooms.

Oscar turned in his chair. "Oh, Jake, baby, you're not allowed to leave your cube without permission from her highness, Nicole."

"Has she even shown up?" Jake asked irritably. Since when did a grown man need permission to go to the bathroom?

"Did you see the woman with ink black hair, black lips and black clothes that came by about an hour ago?"

"The one that looked like Morticia Adams?" The woman had crept eerily down the aisle, then back up again, not saying a word to anyone.

"That's the one. That's Nicole."

"Where is she now?"

Oscar shrugged and turned away as another call came on his line.

"Forget Nicole." Jake had to go. "If she needs me, tell her she's welcome to look in the men's room." He headed down the aisle and turned right toward the tiled hallway. Efficiently, he went through the motions of relieving his bladder, all the while thinking of Charlotte White. What were the odds that she would call tonight? That Jake would be the one answering the phone? It was Fate. Pure and simple.

He had her address and phone number indelibly etched in his memory. But now what? Go to her house, ring the doorbell and, *if* she opened it, ask, "What the hell were you thinking, sending me to jail?" Or maybe he wouldn't say anything. Just showing up, then leaving without saying a word would make her squirm for sure. *It's more likely she'd call the police and put your behind back in jail.*

Shaking off the thought, Jake finished his business and washed his hands. Immediately outside the restroom he encountered the gothic Nicole. Her skin was ghostly white against the abnormally black hair framing her face and the heavy-handed black liner encircling her dark brown eyes. "Were you looking for me?" Jake asked, prepping for a confrontation.

Nicole stared at him vacantly for a moment. "I don't even know you," she finally answered.

"I know. I'm Jake Masters, this is my first day. Didn't Lela tell you about me?"

Nicole's eyes narrowed to heavily outlined slits. "She sent you to watch me," she said in an accusatory whisper. "She did, didn't she?"

Feeling devilish, Jake narrowed his eyes and whispered back, "How did you guess?"

Nicole nodded slowly. "I knew it. But you're not going to find it, you know? You're not good enough."

Jake stood up straight. Now this wayward extra from a horror flick was giving him the creeps. Certain that whatever she was hiding was the last thing he wanted to find, Jake decided to back off. "Don't worry about it. I don't want it."

He took a wide berth around Nicole and headed back toward the mouse maze. He could almost feel her witch eyes burning his backside as he headed down the hallway.

Oscar was coming from the opposite direction. "Bizarre, huh?" he asked, staring straight ahead as he slowed down to talk to Jake.

"Hell, she passed bizarre a few light years ago." Jake kept his voice low and spoke from the side of his mouth. "I think she's landed firmly in Psycholand, my man."

"You got that right," Oscar acknowledged. "I hope she doesn't plan on stopping me. I'd hate to have to piss on her nice black slacks." He pushed onward toward the restroom.

Jake settled back into his chair and adjusted his headphones. The thought of finding Charlotte pressed at his consciousness for a moment before Jake fought it back. He'd have time later to decide what the next step was. In the meantime, he had to make some money to get Shay off his back.

Shay. She'd been all business again this morning, but he could tell the edges of her icy wall were beginning to melt. How long would it take before she let him in?

Chapter Seven

Anticipation took root in Jake's stomach and rose to his head like a helium flower. It was dusk. This had become his time.

He stood watching traffic below from the front window of the apartment. He couldn't wait for the lights of the city to appear and to watch darkness transform the gray, concrete city into a dazzling, neon-rainbowed playground. Surprisingly, Jake actually enjoyed sleeping the day away and working through the night. The dark made everything, even work, so much more mysterious and adventurous than the mundane activities of the day.

The ding of the elevator sounded in the distance and no-nonsense footsteps gained prominence as they clicked along the tiled hallway. The heady helium feeling gave way to a more intense pleasure. A smile formed as the footsteps stopped in front of his door. Shay was home.

It shouldn't excite him the way it did. The woman was as beautiful as a rose, but her personality was thick with thorns.

In their two months together he'd had to carefully

navigate her picky dislikes and moodiness to reveal her softer side. But it was in those fleeting glimpses that Jake found himself captured by how truly magnificent she was.

He wasn't in love with her. He was certain of that. Mostly certain. He liked soft, feminine, flirty women who thrived on attention and waited on him hand and foot. After his last ten years, he deserved a woman like that.

Shay was not that woman.

Lately, she'd become increasingly closed-lipped about what was happening at work. Something big was going on, Jake could tell, but she brushed off his attempts to find out more. Was damned near rude about it. So why the hell did his heart skip as her keys tinkled outside the door?

Shay rushed inside, interrupting whatever revelation Jake was about to have. She tossed her coat, hat and gloves onto the couch, dropped her briefcase to the floor, stepped out of one high heel, then the other as she made a beeline for the kitchen. She had her head inside the refrigerator before the front door slammed solidly shut.

Jake crossed his arms and leaned against the wall near the window. He watched, half-amused, half-concerned, as Shay yanked the half-empty bottle of Merlot from the fridge, uncorked it and gulped down the entirety of its contents without taking a breath. "Thanks for sharing," he jested.

"Where the hell did you come from?" Shay whirled around, her eyes wide as she quickly wiped drops of wine from her mouth and chin.

"Been here the whole time." He pushed away from the wall and walked toward the kitchen. "Nice of you to notice.

"Oh," she said dismissively, and then returned to the refrigerator.

It was clear this wouldn't be the night for humor. "If you're looking for more wine, I believe that was the last of it."

Shay gave him an icy glare and dropped the package of thawed pork chops onto the counter with a thud. "It's my night to cook." Her tone was chilly.

"My bad," he offered by way of apology. Jake placed folded arms on top of the counter and braced himself for Shay's reaction before even asking the question, "How was work today?"

"Same as always." Her forehead wrinkled slightly as she rinsed the meat under running water.

That wasn't too bad. At least she'd given him an answer of sorts. "Testing for the project back on track?" he pressed.

"Not exactly." She pulled Italian breadcrumbs from the

cabinet and large sandwich bags from a drawer.

Jake realized with delight that she was making her un-fried pork chops for dinner. It had fast become one his favorite entrees. Quickly putting aside thoughts of his now rumbling stomach, he tried once again to get Shay to open up. "So how's Cutter taking the delay? Still his old cheerful self?" He knew from previous conversations that Angelo Cutter wasn't a patient man, or one of Shay's favorite people.

"Listen, Jake," Shay shook her head, "I don't want to talk about it, okay?"

Maybe it took being in jail for ten years to appreciate how vulnerable she must feel to keep her needs and wants so completely to herself. Jake knew how hard it was to fight every battle alone. It had taken him two years before he'd asked anyone for help in jail. The alliances he'd finally made, they could hardly be considered friendships, had kept him alive and somewhat sane until his release.

Yet now, it seemed he was in confinement once again. His mother didn't want to talk to him, his attempt to locate his sister in the New Jersey phone book and his brother's address book had been futile, and he no longer had Jerome.

Grief squeezed his heart in its cold grip. Jake felt completely and entirely alone. The only connection he had to his old life was standing before him and she seemed to be fighting his need for closeness with every ounce of her strength.

Jake decided to reach out anyway. "Next week is my birthday."

Shay frowned and continued to prepare their dinner. "I know."

A little surprised, Jake continued, "I was wondering if you'd do me a favor." He rounded the counter to stand next to her at the stove.

Her frown deepened. "What?" she asked cautiously.

"Jerome and I had this thing we did…kind of a ritual." His throat thickened with emotion, forcing him to take a deep breath before going on.

Shay bit her bottom lip and her movements stiffened.

Jake could tell he was making her uncomfortable, but continued. "We…uh…we always gave each other our favorite dessert with a single candle and made a wish for one another. I was wondering if you would go with me to…to Ground Zero on our birthday and…and…" Jake couldn't say anymore. Dropping his head, he squeezed his eyes shut against the sting of tears.

He felt Shay's hand on his upper arm.

"I'll think about it, okay, Jake?" she sounded a bit desperate. "Next Sunday, right?"

Sucking in a huge breath, Jake brought his emotions under control. "Yeah. The fifteenth," he acknowledged. Looking into her brown eyes, he read discomfort mingled with compassion.

"Thanks, Shay." He touched her face then, letting his fingers tell her of his desire to be with her—to be a part of her—to be one with her. Her cheek was warm, soft and the color of the sands on a tropical beach.

Shay's eyes widened as he pushed back her wild ringlets and traced the line of her jaw. He felt the rapid pulse in her neck and then the stiff set of her shoulder still covered with the satiny material of her work blouse.

Jake wondered if kissing her would make her melt wantonly into his arms or have her running like a scared rabbit back to her own room. Her pale pink lips were slightly parted, her breathing shallow.

Deciding not to risk putting more distance between them, Jake let his hand drop to his side. "I guess I'd better get ready for work now."

"Yeah." Shay nodded and seemed relieved. "Okay."

She returned to her cooking as if it were her life's mission.

Jake showered and changed into his work clothes, which now consisted of a clean shirt, a sweater and pressed pair of khakis. He couldn't seem to reconcile himself to wearing jeans and tennis shoes to work just yet. Besides, in a strange twist of fate, Nicole, the psycho, had failed to come to work the previous week and Lela had promoted Jake to supervisor for the shift. He wanted to look a little authoritative.

To his delight, Cleo was in the kitchen with Shay when he emerged from his room. As was her habit, she appeared for dinner when there was no hot dating prospect in her life. "Hey handsome!" She placed her soda can on the counter where she'd been leaning and greeted Jake with a big hug and loud smack on his cheek. "Shay tells me you've been promoted already?"

"I have," Jake replied proudly, allowing Cleo to wipe her lipstick from his face in affectionate strokes.

"I always knew you were hot stuff." She cut her green contact eyes at him flirtatiously and trailed her fingers along his chest before returning to her perch opposite Shay in the kitchen.

"Compared to you, lady, I'm just a steak waiting to sizzle." Jake watched as Cleo soaked up his flattery with an ever-broadening smile on her still dark cherry-colored lips.

"What brings you our way, sweetheart?"

"I heard there was some excitement in Shay's department today and I came to get the scoop." Cleo looked only half-playful as she glanced toward Shay's back.

Jake watched Shay's face as she stirred her macaroni and cheese. The frown returned with a vengeance, plunging her pretty features into an angry mask. She said nothing. Looked thorny.

Time to change the subject, Jake decided. "I don't know about you two, but I'm starving." He rubbed his palms together and headed for the cabinet next to Cleo. "Want to get some glasses, Cleo? I'll put the plates on the table."

"Sure." Cleo's sober eyes met Jake's for a moment. Concern darkened her eyes despite the vivid green of her contact lenses. She was here because she was worried about Shay.

After dinner, Jake and Cleo sat making idle chitchat while Shay washed dishes. It was Jake's turn to do the dishes since Shay had cooked, but for some reason she'd insisted on taking the task anyway.

Cleo told funny stories about people she'd met at her Las Vegas conference. But while her voice remained light and humorous, the same qualities failed to show in her eyes. Jake knew she had more to share, but couldn't while Shay was within earshot.

Shay remained quiet most of the evening, only participating in the conversation when they forced her to do so.

"Much as I hate to leave, Cleo, my love," Jake gave a shrug of regret to let her know he sensed she had more to tell him, "I've got to get to work early tonight."

"I do like a man who takes charge," Cleo offered in her most seductive tone.

Jake went to his room to retrieve his wallet. "Oh, I have something for you, Jake," Cleo called from the next room. Before he could leave his bedroom, she was inside. She nearly closed the door and lowered her voice as she approached him with her business card. "I was wondering if we could meet tomorrow over drinks." All humor and flirtatiousness was gone from her tone and demeanor. "I'm worried about Shay."

Jake nodded and placed the card in his wallet. "I am too. Where do you want to meet?"

"My cell phone number is on the card. Give me a call tomorrow and we'll decide."

"All right."

Cleo was out in the hallway the next second, laughing as if

they'd just shared the best joke.

Jake smiled as he left the room. God bless the woman. She was a great person and friend.

❀

Shay couldn't get rid of Cleo fast enough. The moment the door closed behind her, Shay grabbed her coat and purse and headed for the liquor store, cursing her soon to be ex-friend all the way.

How dare Cleo flirt with Jake so boldly right in front of her? And how dare he flirt right back? They'd acted as if Shay wasn't even in the room. It was rude.

Shay strode inside the liquor store with purpose. She knew exactly what row the wine was in and made quick work of selecting three bottles of her favorite. It took forever for the bald old Korean man to ring up her purchase and impatience and irritability had her shifting from one foot to the other.

The old guy handed her her bag with a "tanka yu" and a slight bow of his head just as Shay's internal clock chimed on eternity.

Shay snatched the bag from his hands, noting his frown of disapproval. Maybe it was rude, but he deserved it for keeping her waiting so long. She pushed out the door and her anger transformed into a rising panic. A caged tiger seemed to be pacing her insides and forced her to sprint the four blocks back to her apartment. She entered her home and shut the door, vowing to lock and deadbolt it in just a few minutes.

"Just a few minutes," she repeated out loud.

Her hands shook as they struggled with the aluminum wrap encasing the top of the bottle. She removed it in three long strips, dropping each to the floor on her way to the kitchen. "I'll pick it up later," she whispered through dry lips, her eyes focused on the cork that lay in her way.

The corkscrew wasn't in the kitchen drawer where she always kept it. She pulled the drawer out further until it stopped abruptly and rattled the silverware. "Damn you, Jake." She spun in a panicked circle, trying to figure out where he would have put it. "The dishwasher," she decided. The man had no problem loading dishes but never put them away.

To her relief, the utensil was lying on the top shelf in plain sight, but removing the cork became an exercise in frustration as the corkscrew only managed to break off tiny pieces of the stopper. Hot tears streamed Shay's face until finally, she was able to pull the obstruction from the bottle.

"Oh, thank God." She sniffed against her now running nose and tilted the bottle with two hands against her anxious lips. She gulped down the dark liquid greedily until her straining lungs forced her to take a breath.

And still there was no relief.

The tiger clawed merciless trails of need and depression deep into her gut. Her knees gave way, forcing her to the floor. Shay held tight to her bottle with one hand, and her aching midsection with the other. Her mouth fell open to cries that were desperate for release, but failed to emerge. Just as with all her wants and needs, the sounds of her pain remained wrapped tight within.

Why was this happening to her? Why wouldn't the pain go away? It was as if the world were conspiring to cause her misery and for a moment, she thought of killing herself.

The thought took hold in some conscious part of her brain and her quiet sobs subsided. At the very least, she could control this one thing—she could plan and execute her own death and no one could stop her. She would have peace…and she would be with Jerome.

"Suicide," she whispered hopefully.

"Suicide," she repeated with a frown. Saying it out loud

changed the whole thing. It had seemed so perfect when it had only been a thought, but the spoken word was ugly and dark. Not at all what she wanted.

No. What she wanted was love and light and happiness...and all the things she thought Jerome could've given her if he'd lived. All the things she'd begun to think Jake could give her...but it was too late.

Jake asked all the time about her day, about her dreams, about herself. She'd been so comfortable talking with him over the past two months, telling him things she hadn't told to anyone else, except maybe Cleo. But she'd always held back on telling him everything. It didn't concern him, she'd told herself. He's only asking to be polite, she'd reasoned. And so, she'd never told him the worst or best things about herself.

But why?

"Because you're an idiot, Shay Bennett." Slowly, she forced herself to her feet and trudged toward her bedroom. "You make the same mistakes over and over."

Jake and Cleo were making plans to see each other. She could tell. Cleo thought she was slick, saying she needed to give Jake something and following him into his room that evening.

Shay knew what she'd given him. A kiss and a quick feel of her newly reconstructed breasts.

"I hope they felt like bricks," she spat, tipping the bottle once more. But knew that they hadn't. She'd poked them herself, at Cleo's insistence, and was surprised at how real they'd felt.

Besides, what right did she have to begrudge Cleo or Jake a little sexual tryst? Cleo liked men. No. Cleo loved men. And Jake was a man, after all. One who hadn't been with a woman for ten years. It would stand to reason that he had needs. Needs she'd read in his eyes more and more often. This evening, for instance, he'd been within a pulse of kissing her. And she'd wanted it so badly.

Closing her eyes, Shay put a hand over her cheek, lay back against her pillow and remembered how wonderful his fingers had felt as they'd caressed her there. Then she imagined Jake's warm, strong hands stroking her body once more. Soothingly, erotically, his hands moved in miraculous circles on her bottom and inside her thighs. If he were here now, she would encourage him, let him know that she was willing to give all of herself to him. If he were here now, she would warm his bed and let him know he had no reason to pursue Cleo.

But he wasn't here now and it was too late. She should have kissed him before Cleo arrived. Shoulda, coulda, woulda, she scolded herself.

Moving a hand to her breast, Shay pressed her palm over the tattooed tears she'd had sculpted there over a month ago. It seemed that the burly man was scraping her skin raw once again with his needle. She could almost smell the stale cigarettes on his clothes and beard as his calloused hands dug into the tender flesh of her breasts. She'd suffered his touch and his smell. Suffered the feeling of the needle scraping her flesh, suffered in silence the way she did all other pain.

Living with Jake was like living with Jerome all over again and Shay wasn't sure that her heart would survive the heartbreak. Finishing the bottle, she dropped it to the floor and went to the kitchen for another. Her hands were much steadier now as she removed the outer wrap and the cork expertly. Carrying the bottle in her arms like a cherished child, Shay returned to her bedroom.

The liquid slowly relaxed her. The tiger retracted its claws and pain and panic dissipated into the darkness of oblivion. Shay floated on the darkness, breathed deeply, sighed her relief and slowly let her head drift into the soft arms of drunken bliss.

Chapter Eight

Jake hurried to the little coffee house on 115th Street, knowing that Cleo wouldn't have much time to talk since she was on her lunch hour. His concern for Shay had grown tenfold that morning and he wanted to speak with Cleo about it.

When he'd returned from work that morning, the apartment smelled of stale alcohol and looked a mess, by Shay's standards. Panicked to find the front door unlocked, Jake had run to her bedroom and found Shay still in bed at a time she was normally at work.

Jake had kicked past two empty wine bottles near her bed to examine her for signs of injury, but she didn't seem hurt. As he'd leaned over to see if she was breathing, the stale smell of alcohol had nearly knocked him to his butt.

Equal amounts of relief and anger had fought within Jake. He'd been a little gruff as he roused her from sleep and forced her to get ready for work. Her reluctance to unravel herself from the twisted sheets and blankets unnerved him. It was scary to see her so complacent and empty of fire.

When she'd finally left their apartment, Shay's head had been down, her shoulders slumped and her footsteps lethargic instead of purposeful as she'd walked toward the elevator. It had taken him all of one minute to find Cleo's business card and give her a call.

Jake entered the cafe and searched anxiously for Cleo. She waved from her seat near a window. Navigating past the small groups of people in their business attire, Jake made his way to the table and slid into the chair gratefully. "Hey, Cleo," Jake said. "You in a hurry?"

"I've got a full staff of managers today. I have time." Cleo pushed a menu in front of Jake. "I know what I'm having."

Jake waved a hand back and forth over the menu. "I'm not hungry." He looked up at the waiter who had just approached. "I'll just have iced tea," he said.

"Cobb salad," Cleo said. She leaned over the table. "So tell me what's got you so upset?"

"It's Shay."

"No kidding." Cleo gave him a "that's obvious" look.

Jake continued. "She's been drinking a lot lately. Last night she downed two bottles of wine after we left. Homegirl smelled like one of those street people when I woke her up."

Cleo's forehead wrinkled. "I've had my suspicions. Does she drink every night?"

"No. But when she does, she goes all out."

Cleo gave a short laugh. "Woman after my own heart."

"Seriously, Cleo," Jake pleaded. "You're worried about her, too. I can tell."

Cleo sighed, nodded. "I am. At work yesterday, I heard that Cutter threatened her job during a teleconference. He called her incompetent in front of her managers and the client heard every word. Apparently my girl gave back as good as she got, but still..." Cleo gave a helpless gesture. "I tried to talk to her about it last night before you came out of your room, but she just said it was nothing. If it were nothing, her section managers wouldn't have been spreading it around the building like butter on hot toast."

"Why does she do that?" Jake sat back in frustration as the waiter placed his tea before him. "I thought she'd at least open up to you."

"Nope. Always been closed in. She'll share something about herself once in a great while, but mostly she just let's me go on and on about myself." Cleo looked at him sheepishly. "Case you didn't notice, I'm full of myself."

Jake smiled. "Maybe we all should be more full of ourselves. Then it wouldn't matter so much what other people think."

"That's one way to look at it," Cleo sighed. "I was thinking you're the best solution for my girl, Shay."

"Me?"

"Yeah." Cleo sat back in her chair and narrowed her heavily-lined eyes. "I see the way you look at her."

Jake heated from his chest to the top of his head. "How do I look at her?"

"Like you wanna sop her up with a biscuit." Cleo smacked her lips for emphasis.

Embarrassment made Jake smile. "I'll try to watch how I look at her from now on."

"Why? I think it's cute."

Jake shook his head and took a long sip of tea. "She keeps me at arm's length. I think she's still in love with Jerome."

"Puhleeze." Cleo rolled her eyes. "Shay wasn't in love with Jerome."

"She said—"

"She was in love with the thought of being in love. Jerome was simply the man in closest proximity."

"How do you know?"

Cleo took her time answering.

Jake found himself moving closer to the edge of his seat.

"Because I've seen the way she looks at you," came her sincere reply. "It's nothing like it was with Jerome. She wanted him because so many other women did."

"She told you this?" Jake asked.

"No." Cleo pushed back her long braids. "But a woman starts to wonder about herself when she turns thirty and has never been in love. She starts to wonder what's wrong with her and why she can't seem to find Mr. Right." She looked reflectively into the glass of water before her and started to trace a line down the moist surface. "Before she knows it, she makes someone Mr. Right, convinces herself completely that she's in love and that this is the man she wants to marry. She doesn't realize until later, sometimes years later, that she's tricked herself."

The intimate way she told the story made Jake wonder if Cleo had done exactly what she spoke of. "Does it happen a lot?" he asked.

"Sugar, they make movies about this stuff," Cleo laughed. "I think they're meant to be instructional, but I'm not sure that's widely known."

The waiter arrived with her salad, giving both of them time

to digest life and love according to Cleopatra Roberts.

"You sure pay a lot of attention to everything going on around you for a woman who's full of herself." Jake pulled a strip of grilled chicken from her plate, suddenly regretting not having ordered food. "So what are we going to do about Shay?" he asked, popping the morsel into his mouth.

Cleo blew out a long breath. "Since we both came here today looking for answers from one another, I don't think we're going to solve that problem today, Jake." She dug into her salad with that.

Jake's stomach grumbled with jealousy. It only took a minute to flag down the waiter, but it took ten for the young man to lope lazily over to their table. "I decided to have a cheeseburger and fries."

The young man made a noise with his tongue and wrote down the order. "Will there be anything else?" he asked with a little attitude.

"I'll let you know," Jake answered with a big smile, deciding he'd ask for dessert later just to irritate the boy.

Cleo giggled and wiped a drop of dressing from her lip. "You're bad."

Jake tapped on the table a little and hummed a nameless tune as he watched Cleo.

She took a sip of water and lifted an eyebrow before asking, "What?"

Jake pursed his lips and wondered if he should ask the question pressing against the back of his mind. Deciding he would burst if he didn't, he shifted in his seat and tucked his head against his chin before asking, "Do you think I really have a chance with Shay?"

He managed to completely mangle the straw cover he picked up from the table before Cleo finally answered.

"Maybe." A thoughtful look was on her face.

"What the hell kinda answer is that?" Jake asked irritably. He'd wanted a solid "yes" or "no." Not a "maybe."

"I don't know why Shay keeps all her feelings locked up so tight. I know she doesn't know who her father is and that she couldn't stand her mother, but I don't know much about her other than that. It occurs to me that it took her a lifetime to build those walls around her heart and there may be pieces I'm missing. But you've known her all her life, grew up with her."

"Yeah. So?"

"So maybe if you put your mind to it, you could find a way to bring down those walls by helping her heal the wounds of her past, Jake."

"I've been trying. I think I might have had a brick or two fall, but other than that—"

"It's going to take a sledge hammer, man." She gave him a look as serious as a heart attack. "Maybe even a wrecking ball. You tend to be soft and gentle, Jake, but that won't do the trick. You have to find a strength equal to hers and make her deal with your feelings—and her own."

"I'm not one to force myself on anyone, Cleo."

"I didn't say rape her."

Jake bristled and gave Cleo a hard look.

"Sorry," she backed off. "I just meant that if you make the first move, that might be all it takes."

Jake had to admit that he'd thought the same thing from time to time. "You might be right," he acquiesced. "I'll think about it." He sat up as the waiter meandered around tables to bring his meal.

"Think long, think wrong," Cleo sang with a smile.

Feeling his mood lighten with her teasing, Jake dug into his food with renewed appetite and decided he'd satisfy his appetite for Shay sooner rather than later.

"You're a wise woman, Cleopatra," he said with a big bite of burger tucked between his cheek and tongue.

Her smile turned wicked. "Oh waiter," she called just as

the boy started to leave.

"Yeah?" He pushed strands of his gold-tipped black hair from his face with impatience.

"Could I get a slice of cheesecake, please?" She handed her empty salad plate to him.

Red splotches colored the boy's neck as he snatched her plate and stormed off on feet too large for his skinny body.

❁

Charlotte didn't know at first if she'd taken one too many lines of coke earlier or if she'd actually seen Jacob Masters walk through the door of the café. Her heart palpitated skittishly as she'd watched him scan the room and then take off down the other side of the restaurant. Only a few weeks ago, she'd thought the man taking her order on the phone sounded like Jake, now she was seeing him in person.

It couldn't be. She wrinkled her brow trying to remember the judge's sentence ten years ago. Jake wouldn't be up for parole for another five years, she was certain. But damned if that man hadn't looked just like him.

It hit her then. Jacob Masters had a twin brother. He'd been at the trial every day. She couldn't remember his name.

"Aren't you going to finish your sandwich, sweetheart?" Damian interrupted her thoughts while pulling out his cell phone to accept an incoming call.

Charlotte didn't bother to answer since he was now talking to whomever was on the other end of the call. She pushed aside the remainder of her turkey sandwich as her resentment at having to be with him grew. Despite his insistence that he missed her horribly when he was working, he stayed in constant contact with his office when he was supposedly spending quality time with her. She knew he was trying to keep her on a short leash by asking her to lunch three times a week.

Disgust churned her stomach like sour milk as she watched her husband dictating orders to one of his associates while covering her hand possessively. She wanted to be anywhere but in his presence. Pulling her hand from beneath his, Charlotte placed her napkin on the table and mouthed that she was going to the restroom.

He nodded his understanding and continued to discuss actions needed for the client accused of double homicide.

"Sure, free another guilty thug," she murmured.

As she rounded a post, she spotted the man again. Jake's twin was sitting near the window with a chocolate-dark woman wearing a cheap suit. She wondered if they were involved, but then decided that it hardly mattered. The man was viciously handsome. Enough to test the limit of Damian's patience, she hoped. And he was the brother of the man she'd had convicted of rape.

Charlotte bit her bottom lip anxiously and slowed her step. To get to the restroom she'd have to walk past his table. She wondered if he would recognize her. What if he did?

Charlotte took a deep breath and moved forward. When she reached his table, she paused until she'd caught his attention. There was a gleam of recognition in his sexy brown eyes that made her insides churn anxiously. Quickly she turned and entered the ladies' restroom.

Breathing a little quicker now, Charlotte checked her image in the mirror. Perfect. Her makeup was flawless, as usual, but no amount of cosmetics could hide the ugly feelings she carried inside.

A decade ago, pretending to be drunker than she really was, she'd selected Jake Masters from the club and taken him home. Even ten years later, she'd give the man's sexual performance a gold medal. He'd made love to her as if he cared, made her slow down, enjoy the feeling of his skillful hands. His long, slow strokes had made her light-headed. She'd thought on many occasions what a waste he was in jail. She was sorry that she'd had to do what she did. But there was no helping it. She wondered if Jake's brother would understand or if he would even give her an opportunity to apologize.

Flipping long strands of her weave over her shoulder, Charlotte prepared to re-introduce herself to the second Mr. Masters. If she could get inside his house, she might get an opportunity for redemption.

Jake stared at the women's restroom door in disbelief. He'd managed to push the thought of Charlotte White to the back of his consciousness for the past two weeks, but now she was here, in the flesh, and looking just as hot as ever.

"Yo, Jake!" Cleo waved a hand in front of his eyes. "You don't want no part a that. That's trouble walking if I ever saw it."

"I know." Jake downed the remainder of his drink in a quick gulp. "That woman put me in jail for ten years."

"Her?"

Jake nodded.

Cleo looked at him quizzically. "Then why was she giving you the come on? Seems awfully bold."

Shrugging, Jake couldn't explain her actions any more than

he could the sudden rush of hormones raging through his veins. He had to be insane to still be attracted to a woman who'd lied to put him behind bars.

She emerged from the restroom at that moment, looking like all that had been forbidden since the beginning of time. Jake's manhood jerked to attention, ignoring the warning bells in his brain. Charlotte was wearing a halter top and a pair of slacks that formed to her hips and booty like Saran Wrap. She looked better than he'd remembered.

Her smile was full of sugar as she approached their table. With no acknowledgement whatsoever to Cleo, she placed a beautifully manicured hand, sporting a fat diamond ring on the table. "Don't I know you from somewhere?" she asked Jake innocently.

It wasn't possible that she'd forgotten who he was. Jake tried to tell himself he should be irritated, but couldn't quite find the emotion beneath the high buzz of his frenzied hormones. "If you're Charlotte White, I believe we had a brief encounter about ten years ago." He tried to make the comment bite.

She beamed brightly. "I thought so. You're Jacob Masters' twin brother, right?"

Of course, Jake thought. She wouldn't have been nearly so

bold if she'd known it was really him. Of course, to make a move on his twin brother was nearly as bad. "Yeah," he said, not knowing why he didn't just come out with the truth. "Jerome Masters." He offered his hand and sent a warning glance toward Cleo.

To her credit, Cleo remained as cool as spring rain.

"This is my friend—"

"Cleo Roberts." Cleo offered a hand to the woman.

Charlotte murmured something dismissively. "Do you live around here, Jake?" Her light brown eyes were hopeful. There was no mistake that she was offering him the gift of sex as she leaned forward to let him gaze upon the soft sway of her breasts beneath the scarf she was using as a blouse.

Jake felt like a mouse hypnotized by the seductive sway of a cobra's stare. He swallowed hard against the dryness in his throat. "Not far."

"You should call me." She slid a card across the table at him. "I've gotta go now, but I'd love to do you tomorrow."

"Do me?" He could hardly believe his ears.

"Oops. I meant do lunch." She wiggled her fingers and giggled as she strode away.

"She meant what she said the first time," Cleo scoffed just loud enough for the retreating woman to hear. "What's on that card that heifah gave you, Jake?" She pulled it from beneath his now moist fingers.

It was a black card with white letters that simply said Charlotte White with a phone number listed. It wasn't the same number he'd committed to memory, though. Maybe it was a cell phone.

"I do not believe this. That ho just left you with a stiff one knocking against the table to go back to her date. I'll bet a million bucks the guy with the cell phone is her husband." Cleo was straining to see over the crowd to watch Charlotte.

"It's definitely her husband," Jake offered, taking a good look at the man who'd defended Charlotte's lies to the jury in his case. Damian White had a cell phone glued to his ear and seemed oblivious to everything around him.

Jake shook his head and turned back to Cleo. "Am I imagining things or did she just proposition me in front of God and everybody?" Jake asked.

"Technically," Cleo lifted an eyebrow, "she propositioned your brother."

Jake waved off her comment as he would a nagging fly. "It might be fun to string her along," he offered by way of explanation, still not completely certain why he'd lied.

"If I were you, I wouldn't touch that," Cleo warned sternly. "That woman has serious issues."

Jake couldn't argue that point. One thing was certain, it would be impossible to keep Charlotte White in the back of his mind any longer.

❖

Shay was frozen outside her office building, dreading the three steps that would take her inside. Looking skyward, she let the soft flakes of snow kiss her face. It felt real, the snow and the icy breeze that whirled them into a frenzied dance before allowing them to land gently on her cheeks, nose and lips. So real that she didn't feel guilty that people were walking around her to get inside.

The sounds of taxis honking, tires sloshing and footsteps trudging through sandy brown slush that had once been a pristine powdery white blanket were harsh against the low clouds of the gray skies. The wind pushed through the collar of her coat and penetrated the tiny holes in her knit cap to chill her skin. Her gloved fingers and booted toes were stiff as ice sculptures. Still, she would trade standing out here forever to going inside and facing another day of work.

Shay brought her eyes down from the sky and stared at the

revolving doors before her. One thing was for sure: the day would never be over if she didn't first get it started.

Pushing out a noisy breath, Shay entered the glass and steel building. She enjoyed the relatively peaceful ride up in the elevator, knowing it would be the only solace she'd have all day.

Sometimes, Shay hated to be right.

The moment she reached her seventh floor office, things quickly heated up. Ray and Chase were in her office complaining about more problems with the Blue Banana software. Team Dynamics called to set up another status meeting by teleconference. The only agenda item they had was to discuss pulling out of the project and going with another company. Everything would've been all right if Angelo hadn't been in there making everything seem ten times worse than it was. And then to call her incompetent in front of their client...

Shay pushed the thought aside. It only made her angry and incapable of clear thought. The one thing she needed desperately today was a clear head.

Sydney had walked into Shay's office before she'd had the first sip of coffee, that she'd finally managed to find time to buy in the cafeteria.

Sydney handed Shay a letter and said two words: "I quit."

Shay stared at the woman in disbelief.

Sydney sat calmly, resolutely, in the chair opposite Shay, just as serene as if she were sitting in the park on a sunny day.

"You can't quit, Sydney. Not now," Shay insisted, pushing aside the resignation letter. "I need you. The project needs you."

Sydney removed the thick black-framed glasses. For the first time, Shay noticed the bags and tiny age lines beneath the woman's eyes. "Listen, Shay. I was going to retire in a few years anyway. To be honest with you, I don't appreciate the way you ride me and everyone else around here. It's not worth staying if I'm to be treated as if I were a child."

"I don't treat you like a child, Sydney," Shay shot back. "I may be direct, but that's just because I like things to get done when I need them to be done. Now, if you're too sensitive—"

"Wait a minute now." Sydney had a hand in the air, waving it back and forth with a purpose. "I've been through two bad marriages and the teenage years of four children. I gave up being sensitive twenty years ago. I'm talking about respect. You don't respect me."

Shay was surprised at the bright, blazing anger in the older woman's eyes. "I do respect you, Syd. I think you're a great manager and one of the best problem solvers on our team. That's why I need you."

"Respect doesn't yell at a person when something out of their control goes wrong. Respect doesn't ask for updates on things that a person hasn't even had a chance to start. Respect doesn't threaten the jobs of people who need them."

"Give me a break, Sydney. You see what Angelo does to me. I've been threatened in front of my customers and my employees, but I don't sit here feeling sorry for myself."

"Is that what you think I'm doing?" Sydney looked indignant. "Feeling sorry for myself?"

Shay began to feel sick to her stomach.

Sydney rose from her chair. "I understand you're trying to be as strong as the men in this company, Shay. And I know that's a tough thing to do." Her voice was kind, but unyielding. "But there's a difference in being tough and in being wrong."

"Is it so wrong to work hard and expect everyone else to work just as hard?" Shay asked, deflated. Her fingers were tingling and she was slightly lightheaded. She should have eaten breakfast, she decided. "I try to walk the walk and work the problems right along with all of you. I do this to have my employees…to have you…respect me."

"You and I both know that respect can't be forced. It's earned. Tell me how much respect you have for Angelo Cutter," Sydney pressed.

"He's a brilliant man—" Shay began half-heartedly.

"That doesn't excuse poor behavior. And you know it. I'm not quitting because the work is hard, Shay. I'm quitting because I've lost faith in the people I work for." Sydney strode out of the office with her head held high.

"Wait, Sydney…" Shay dropped her head to the desk with a thud and uttered a profanity into the stack of papers beneath her face. "I knew I should've stayed in bed." Queasiness had her stomach roiling and her jaws tingling. Her temples throbbed and Shay gave serious thought to taking a sick day. But there was still a job that needed to get done.

Sydney's quitting was just the tip of the iceberg. She had to realign the employees with the other two managers and oversee the remainder of the testing herself. She put a hand to the phone and stopped. How was she going to tell Angelo Cutter that she'd just lost one of the section managers pivotal to the Team Dynamics project?

"You have something to tell me, Bennett?" Angelo was there—standing in the doorway like the fruition of a bad dream. How could he have found about Sydney so fast? "How did you know?" she asked.

"It's my job to know what's going on at all times." He stepped inside and closed the door behind him viciously. "You're two weeks behind in testing for your project. Two damned weeks! You're not making me happy, Shay." His face was nearly purple, veins had appeared on his forehead and his jaw muscles were so tense they looked chiseled.

Anger gripped Shay, cold and hard, as the man paced her office, stabbing his finger in her direction and ranting like a madman.

"Hold on, Angelo." Shay put up a hand to stop the man's tirade. "You're making a bad situation worse by all of these tantrums you're having—"

"Tantrums?" His eyes turned to slits of red hatred. "Listen, little missy, I've been managing projects since before you graduated from college and I know when a manager has lost control. I'm giving serious consideration to taking over this one myself."

"And do what?" Shay grew more lightheaded as her anger intensified. "The problem we're having is with the specifications we've received from Blue Banana for their old scheduling software. Something's missing and it's making it impossible for us to solve the interface problem."

"What interface problem?"

Shay rolled her eyes. "The problem I was talking about during our meeting yesterday. Our training software interfaces beautifully with the upgraded version of Blue Banana, but crashes with the older version Team Dynamics seems committed to keeping. I was ready to discuss options, Angelo, when you dropped in your two cents about how sorry you were that my team and I weren't competent enough to solve the problem."

"What options?" Angelo challenged.

"Option one, Team Dynamics spends the forty grand it takes to upgrade to the new version of Blue Banana. Option two...," Shay placed a hand to her seriously upset stomach, "...Blue Banana gives us accurate specs on the old software, which they don't want to do because they would prefer that Team Dynamics upgrade. Option three, we continue to work on solving the interface problem with incomplete specs."

"And you chose the last one which was the wrong choice!" Angelo shouted. "How do you expect to solve an interface puzzle when you don't have all the pieces, Bennett?"

Shay saw spots before her eyes. She opened her mouth to tell him that her analysts and programmers had come close to solving the problem, but needed her to do some fast negotiating with Blue Banana on their behalf to get just one more piece of the code. But she couldn't seem to get even the first word out before pain, fast and sharp, pierced her heart and screamed through her chest. She couldn't breathe—couldn't talk—couldn't...

"Bennett?" Angelo's voice seemed to come from another room. She couldn't see him anymore. It was dark.

Chapter Nine

Charlotte knew he'd call. They always did. She took in the magnificent view of Jerome Masters in his red, fitted T-shirt and blue jeans. She reminded herself that this visit wasn't for pleasure. She had to play it cool. "I want you to know I don't get up this early in the morning for just anybody," she said, tapping at her watch, trying to keep their conversation light.

Jerome Masters opened the door wider for her to enter. "It's eleven o'clock." He sounded a little irritated. "I invited you for ten."

Despite the small flare of anger in his dark brown eyes, his clothes-searing gaze told Charlotte his mood could easily be altered. She made a point of brushing against him as she entered his apartment. Her heart pounded hard and fast as if she'd run up the stairs instead of taking the elevator.

"Don't be mad, Jerome." She gave him her best pout. "I had a late night." Unfortunately, Damian hadn't even noticed her slipping Jerome her card at the restaurant. She'd had to push him away all night.

Jerome stepped over to help her out of her coat. "Why don't you have a seat? Are you hungry? I made breakfast."

While he made his way over to the kitchen, Charlotte wandered around the living room. It was small but cozy with oversized furniture and colorful throw pillows. Cheaply decorated, but in good taste. He lived with a woman, she decided. No doubt about it. "That woman you were with yesterday," she asked innocently, "is she your wife?"

"Would it matter?"

There was an edge to his voice that irritated Charlotte. Too many men had used that exact tone with her. "Only if it does to you," she stated matter-of-factly.

Jerome looked up from the food that steamed from two plates on the counter before him. His gaze was unreadable. "She's not."

Clearing her throat, Charlotte tried to toss aside the feeling of uneasiness that had just gripped her. She was supposed to be in control of this situation. He didn't have the right to mess it up with attitude. "She wouldn't be happy that I'm here though, right?"

Jerome shrugged. "Probably not," he said simply. He'd

rounded the tall counter and had placed the plates on the table. A big sipper cup full of fresh flowers stood in the middle of the round table.

"Interesting centerpiece," she stated, taking the seat next to Jerome rather than opposite him. Her tight skirt slid up a couple of inches, exposing the greater part of her thigh. She looked at the ham, fried eggs and hashed browns on her plate, but couldn't find an appetite for food.

It occurred to Charlotte that the only conversation she knew how to have with a man was limited to sexual innuendo. How was she supposed to ask the questions that had haunted her since seeing him yesterday? How's you're brother doing in the pen? Seemed a little abrupt. Still, she had to say something.

"To tell you the truth, Jerome, I'm not real hungry. I wanted..." she took a deep breath, "I wanted to talk with you."

"Talk?" Jake looked at her with cautious eyes. "About what?"

Charlotte twisted the paper napkin he'd provided. "What do you think?"

"Okay." The man leaned back in his chair and crossed his arms. "I'm ready. Apologize."

His tone was judgmental and bossy. Charlotte didn't

appreciate it. "Look, I didn't have to come here," she shot back.

"And I didn't have to invite you," he answered. "But since you seemed hell-bent on grabbing my attention yesterday, I got curious. To be honest, I expected you to try to jump my bones. I never dreamed you'd have this kind of nerve. What kind of apology do you think will be adequate enough to make up for what you've done?"

"Is that what you want? Sex?" Charlotte ran her hand up Jerome's hard thigh, found his zipper and slid it down abruptly. "I can do that too, Jerome. I can give you sex. Will you be willing to listen to me then?"

"Don't do that," he said, dropping an unsteady hand to his plate.

"Why, sugar?" Charlotte stood, threw her leg over his lap angrily and pushed the table back with her behind. "You telling me you're not having fun?" She sank to her knees before him prepared to knock the judgmental tone from his mouth but quick.

Jerome rose from his chair, grabbed her by her upper arms, lifted her and planted her firmly on her feet. "I didn't bring you here for that." His handsome face was now twisted in disgust.

"Could've fooled me." Charlotte crossed her arms angrily and gave a nod toward the erection outlined in his blue silk boxers."

Quickly, Jerome zipped his pants. "I just wanted to see how far you would take this."

"Take what? What are you talkin' about?" she asked, feeling her temper rise.

"All men are to you is something to scratch that insatiable itch between your legs."

She didn't know if it was the partial truth in his words or the fact that her plan to assuage her guilt hadn't worked, but Charlotte knew she'd made a mistake. She'd had no business even trying to find out how Jake was doing. She headed for the couch to retrieve her coat, angrier with herself than Jerome.

"Tell me something, Mrs. White. Do you really feel any guilt for having put an innocent man in jail?"

Charlotte, who was punching her arms into her coat like a heavyweight boxer, stilled as the question hung in the air. She narrowed her eyes and studied the man carefully. "You're Jake Masters, aren't you?" she asked, not quite meeting his eyes.

"Yeah."

"I thought you were still—"

"Bad news, Charlotte." He moved to stand in front of her. His voice dropped to a harsh whisper. "A DNA test proved that I wasn't the one who raped you that night. Which we both know since I was using a condom."

Heavy with the guilt she'd kept locked away for a decade, Charlotte moved to sit on the couch before her knees gave out. "I had to do it, Jake," she said wearily. Now she did meet his bronze gaze. "I was trapped. I couldn't see any other way out and Damian said—"

"Damian your husband?" Jake asked incredulously. "He was in on this beyond representing you?"

Charlotte watched the man's muscles tense to the point of trembling and imagined his closed fists connecting with her face at any moment. "Yes." It was her turn to whisper as emotion stole her voice. "My father was so upset when he came to see me in the hospital. I had to tell him something to explain how my face and ribs got busted up. Daddy wanted someone to pay and I couldn't tell him the truth."

"What was the truth, Charlotte?" Jake's tone was unyielding.

"That I was selling drugs for Machete...and selling myself."

"So what happened?" Jake challenged. "You forgot to pay

this Machete and he raped you and then beat you?"

Nodding, Charlotte leaned back against the couch, growing warm under the wool coat. "Damian was one of my regulars at the time. He wanted me bad. Got jealous anytime I had appointments with other men and got real upset whenever he found Machete's bruises all over me. He was also Machete's lawyer so he cooked up this deal. He promised we'd pin the rape on someone else if Machete agreed to let me go and not hurt my family. In exchange, he asked me to marry him."

Jake felt as if he'd just been dropped into a segment of the Twilight Zone. He turned in a frustrated circle on the hardwood floor as he struggled to understand all the pieces of this complicated puzzle. "So, if all this happened after I left you that night, and I wasn't one of your johns, how the hell did I get wrapped up in all this?"

Blowing out a long breath, Charlotte seemed to search for the answer. "I went to see all my johns that night at hotel rooms or at their houses. I was done working by the time I hit the club and found you. I took you home for fun." She gave a weak smile. "Plus, people had seen us leave the club together, even Damian. He was the one that pointed out that you didn't have an alibi."

Renewed anger had Jake pacing the room. "So it was easiest to pin the whole thing on me," he said rhetorically. "You know, for ten years I woke up when I was told, I ate when I was told, I slept when I was told and I watched my back 24/7. You stole my life because you couldn't tell your Daddy you were a drug dealing whore and because you wanted to marry a rich lawyer."

His words burned like fire inside Charlotte's gut. "It wasn't my fault, Jake."

"It was and is your fault, Charlotte." Jake was nearly nose-to-nose with her now. "You could've chosen to do the right thing."

"Don't you understand?" Charlotte pleaded with him. "I was being beaten daily. I was entangled with a maniac who would not have hesitated to hurt my father, my mother, my sister at the drop of a hat. I had no way out, Jake. No way but Damian's way." Tears filled her eyes. "I feel horrible that you went to jail. I've hated Damian more and more every day for putting away a nice guy who happened to catch my eye.

Jake's compassionate side wanted to forgive her, but anger and disgust won the upper hand as reason said that she still wasn't accepting responsibility for her own actions—past or present. "Damian couldn't have done anything without your testimony," he said angrily.

Her face clouded with frustration. "I've been in a loveless marriage for ten years. My husband defends guilty men successfully on a regular basis. He bought me from my pimp, taking advantage of me when I had no other choices. I loathe his touch."

"You've been released from your prison, Jake. And I'm glad about that. But I have no idea how to get out of mine."

Jake lifted his arms, then let them drop to his side. "Ask for a divorce, Charlotte." He nearly screamed the words at her. "Quit acting like the victim here. You had choices, you just made the wrong ones. You still have choices. If you leave the man, what's the worse that could happen to you?"

"I could end up back in the streets. My parents don't want anything to do with me and I would never go back to Machete."

"Well, you could get a job. It's not that hard." Jake couldn't believe he was having this conversation. How could anyone feel so helpless when there were so many things they could be doing for themselves? "You'd get some money from the divorce, right?"

Charlotte shook her head sadly. "He made me sign a prenuptial agreement. I would barely get anything. He did his best to make sure I couldn't leave him."

"Did you ever think maybe the poor SOB's in love with you too much to think about a divorce?" Jake could tell by her troubled look that the thought had crossed her mind and she didn't find it pleasant. He felt immensely sorry for Damian White for a hot second, but then let the feeling pass. The man had made this bed. He had to lie in it next to the black widow here.

Suddenly Jake was sorry he'd ever called Charlotte. Her explanation hadn't made him any happier though it put some part of him at rest. He knew why she'd done it now. He looked at the woman who suddenly looked old and tired rather than young and vivacious. He wished she'd leave.

The phone rang, breaking the silence that had settled in the room. "Excuse me," Jake said.

Charlotte muttered something that sounded as if she had to go as he lifted the receiver. "Hello?"

"Jake, you have to come right away!"

"Cleo?" Her panicked tone frightened Jake. "What's wrong?"

"It's Shay. She's in the hospital."

Fear made his blood rush and time move slowly. "Where are you now?"

"I'm at Saint Joseph's in the waiting room. They've got her in intensive care. They think she had a heart attack."

"I'm on my way." Jake slammed down the receiver and raced to his room for his coat and gloves. "I've got to go," he said to Charlotte who was already on her way to the door.

"I'll see ya," she said and left.

Jake sincerely hoped not.

By the time he reached the street to hail a cab, Charlotte was nowhere in sight and thoughts of her were replaced by worries about Shay. He'd thought of her often at night when he walked around Manhattan before work, enjoying the joyful life around him. Musicians played on street corners, laughter and conversation spilled from restaurants and bars. Couples and friends walked the streets in lavish nighttime costumes, hurrying to see the new musicals and plays on and off Broadway.

New York was alive and more romantic than he'd remembered. On more than one occasion he'd wondered what it would be like to take Shay out into the night, to have her by his side enjoying the sights, the sounds and the fun. He feared now that he might never have the chance. As he pulled open the door to the cab, he pleaded, "Please God, don't take her, too." He hadn't finished grieving his brother's death. Jake didn't think he could take another loss.

A cold wind blew him inside the cab, along with a flurry of snowflakes. The gray skies heightened Jake's fear. "Saint Joseph's as quick as you can," he instructed the driver. A firm pressure settled on his shoulders then. The weight was comforting and kept him from hurrying the driver who carefully navigated the slushy streets toward their destination.

"Hold on, Shay," he offered as if she could hear him. "I'm coming."

Chapter Ten

Some weird dream about arguing with a blue banana that sounded like Angelo Cutter chased Shay from sleep and into blessed consciousness. The moment her eyes opened she found herself peering into the worried faces of Cleo and Jake. Though they stood on opposite sides of her bed, she couldn't help the stab of hurt that washed over her at the sight of the two of them together. "What's up?" She tried to sit up, but found her arm tangled with tubing that seemed to be growing from the back of her hand.

"Whoa!" Jake put his hands to her shoulders and gently forced her back against the pillows. "You're not going anywhere for a while."

Shay looked around in confusion. Nothing was familiar, not the hard adjustable twin bed, the scratchy sheets, the overstuffed pillows, or the smell of sickness and antiseptic. "I'm in the hospital?" She asked. "What for?"

"You passed out in your office," Cleo explained, grabbing her hand. "Oh, sugar, they thought you had a heart attack."

"A heart attack? I feel fine," Shay insisted. "I probably passed out because I hadn't eaten breakfast or something."

Cleo lifted an eyebrow. "Everyone says you were arguing with Angelo before it happened."

"I always argue with Angelo. But I wouldn't give the man the satisfaction of having a heart attack over him," she said irritably.

"That's my girl!" Jake laughed. "Glad to have you back." He kissed her cheek.

The softness of his lips contrasted with the scratchiness of his stubbled cheek. Shay liked it. Stop it. He belongs to Cleo now, she reminded herself.

"What time is it?" Shay asked, suddenly recalling the disagreement she'd been having with Angelo before unconsciousness so rudely interrupted her. She couldn't allow him to talk with Team Dynamics again. He'd screw the whole project up.

"It's just past noon," Cleo said, consulting her watch.

"Help me find my clothes," Shay ordered her friend. She jumped out of bed before Jake could stop her a second time. "I have work to do and no time to be sitting in a hospital room."

"The doctor hasn't released you yet." Jake rounded the bed

and grabbed her free hand halting her attempt to remove the I.V. from her other hand. "Your work isn't going anywhere."

"Unless you want to be paying all our bills with your tiny paycheck, you'd better move out my way." Shay didn't mean to be harsh, but Jake brought home only half the money she did.

Jake gave her a stern look. "I have the potential to make more money. You don't if you're dead."

His grip remained firm around her wrist. There wasn't even a hint of softness in his eyes. Shay realized with some surprise that the brother meant business.

"Now, get back in the bed. Please," he added, but his tone was anything but polite.

Not knowing what else to do, Shay slowly backed up to the mattress and lay down. Jake pulled the scratchy sheet and thin blanket over her gently while Cleo looked on with a smug grin plastered on her face. Shay sighed and tried not to care. "I don't know why ya'll are trippin'. I didn't have a heart attack."

"You're right. You didn't." Doctor Yvonne von Phul walked into the room in her white lab coat. Her salt-and-pepper hair was pulled into a no-fuss ponytail that hung to her shoulders. Shay had never known her doctor to wear makeup. But then, she didn't seem to need it. Her skin was a deep mocha that was smooth as polished onyx.

The doctor approached Shay's bedside. "You had an anxiety attack. It's not life threatening, but usually feels like it is. The pain made you hyperventilate, which caused your blackout."

Shay nodded. "That about sums it up. When can I go?"

Doctor von Phul shot her a motherly frown. "When I'm satisfied. I haven't gotten all of your test results back yet, but preliminarily there doesn't appear to be anything wrong with your heart. If everything checks out all right, you can go home tomorrow morning."

Shay was horrified. "Tomorrow morning? That's an eternity. Please, Doctor, let me out now and I'll promise to come see you tomorrow at your office. If I stay here the rest of the day I know I'll have another attack."

"If you go back to work, you'll have another attack," Cleo argued.

"Can you work from home?" Jake interjected.

All eyes turned to the man.

Jake shrugged. "I'm home until seven, Doc," he explained. "I could keep an eye on her until I have to go to work."

It was a brilliant solution, Shay decided. As soon as they

left the hospital, she could make her way back to the office and do damage control. "Sure. I can make the calls I need from home," she agreed.

Skepticism lined the older woman's face. "All right. But I expect to see you in my office sometime tomorrow. Schedule an appointment as soon as you get home," she ordered.

"I will." Shay tried to look sincere. The last call she would make today would be to Doctor von Phul's office. The first would be to Team Dynamics.

"I'll have the nurse take out that I.V. and I'll sign your release." The doctor left the room.

Cleo moved to the side of the bed and squeezed Shay's hand. "Since you're in good hands..." she winked at Jake, "I'll go back to work and let them know you're alive and kickin'. Literally."

"Thanks, Cleo." Shay continued her 'good girl' façade. She would make her condition known in person in about a half-hour if the nurse hurried up.

At that moment the nurse whisked into the room cheerfully. "Doctor von Phul says you get to go home. Isn't that fabulous?"

Shay smiled and nodded, holding in her impatience.

Jake moved out of the woman's way as she worked efficiently to remove the I.V. from Shay's hand. "I'll be waiting outside."

"Okay," Shay replied. Once the nurse was finished she nearly jumped from the bed to find her clothes in the small little cubby they called a closet. After she was clothed, she strapped on her watch and checked the time. Three o'clock. The day was nearly over. She'd have to work fast.

Shay shoved her feet into her pumps. Shoot. She had no coat, no hat, no boots. And, to her irritation, her purse wasn't accounted for either. She'd have to borrow money from Jake to catch a cab.

As Shay exited the room, Jake shoved away from the wall he'd been leaning on. "No coat?" he asked.

"Probably didn't think I'd need it in the ambulance." Shay talked as she turned around in the hallway. "How do we get out of here?"

"Follow me." Jake smiled and gallantly offered the crook of his arm.

Shay sighed. "I can walk on my own, Jake."

"So can I," he replied good-naturedly. His arm remained where it was. "Would it be so difficult to allow me to escort you out of here?"

Of course it wouldn't. Plus, if it got them out sooner rather than later... Shay put her arm inside his and let him lead her down the hallway. It was embarrassing to pass the nurse's station and have each of the ladies smile in that ahh-isn't-that-sweet kind of way, then drop their heads. Shay felt extremely self-conscious, but when she looked at Jake, he seemed happy, almost proud, to have her on his arm.

Shay didn't know why, but she was suddenly overcome with the desire to cry. Maybe it was because Jake was so damned sweet. Maybe it was because she was so damned stupid.

They took the elevator to the first floor and stood at the entrance to the front door. Jake took his coat that he'd been carrying and draped it around Shay's shoulders. "Wait here. I'll get a cab," he instructed.

"Jake." Shay stopped him. "We'll need two cabs. I've got to get to work. Could you lend me the cab fare? I'll pay you when I get home."

Jake placed his hands on his hips and stared at her as if she were crazy. "You're coming home with me. That was the deal."

"I only agreed so the doctor would release me. I had every intention of going back to the office. Besides, my purse is there, my coat, my hat—"

"Cleo can get your stuff and bring it to you tonight. You're coming home with me," he reiterated as the iron in his eyes returned. "Make whatever calls you need to make from the apartment." He left then and hailed a cab.

She should've been angry, but Shay couldn't conjure up the feeling. Instead, she stood biting her bottom lip, thinking the man getting pummeled by snowflakes outside was about the sexiest thing on the planet.

Jake jerked out of sleep and forced his eyes to open. They felt red and raw and angry because he wouldn't let them rest. He sat in the overstuffed chair in the living room, watching Shay wheel and deal in their living room.

He'd watched in wonder for the past two hours at how she soothed her customer from Team Dynamics, put fire to the bottoms of her managers, and butted heads with her boss, Angelo Cutter. She was now on the phone with someone from a company called Blue Banana, using the sweetest tone Jake had ever heard.

Though Jake had put a blanket and pillow on the couch for her comfort, Shay had not sat down the entire time they'd been home. Instead, she'd paced the living room with the stealth of a black panther.

Jake was pretty sure she'd forgotten he was even there. He grinned with satisfaction and sank lower into the chair. He let his eyes nearly close as he continued to watch the woman move around the room. She undid another button and the weighty lapels fell to the side, revealing her long neck and the very top of her black bra.

A song played in Jake's mind. One he'd heard at a strip club long ago. It was slow and sensual, like Shay's uninhibited movements. Long ago, she'd abandoned her shoes by stepping out of them. He loved how she'd done that. Now she sat on the arm of the couch, reached beneath her skirt and pushed down her pantyhose bit-by-bit.

Fatigue left him as he let his eyes travel the length of her smooth, sandy brown legs that were up and moving once more. Something primal in him wondered what kind of underwear she was wearing. It was a totally inappropriate thought, but he couldn't help imagining how spectacular she would look in something black and lacey.

As Shay turned to face the back of the room, she shifted sexily from one leg to the other. The music in Jake's mind grew louder as the outline of her firm bottom moved left to right, right to left against the wool of her skirt.

It occurred to Jake that he'd never seen her so free, so passionate and versatile. Her voice was music; her movements, dance. Jake sat amazed and enraptured by his first real glimpse of the woman Shay Bennett was.

An erection pressed hard against his Sean Johns, but Jake didn't move, barely breathed, afraid that any movement would catch Shay's attention and she would stop what she was doing and retreat into her protective walls.

Shay turned his way but looked over Jake's head, totally engrossed in her conversation. Her eyes were ablaze, her face full of color and life as she spoke and gestured. Glimpses of her sienna skin as Shay pulled her blouse from her skirt hastened the music in his mind. The throb in his boxers matched the beat of his striptease and the quickened pace of his heart.

Shay removed the phone from her ear, gave a loud sigh and stretched.

It took all Jake's strength to remain in his chair. "Did you avert the crisis?" He tried to sound casual.

"I thought you were sleeping," Shay said, a little startled as she flopped onto the couch. Her skirt rode up a few inches.

Jake's erection matched the rise.

"I think so. Angelo had almost ruined everything, but I got Team Dynamics calmed down and sweet-talked Drake at Blue Banana into sending us over the missing code. We should be back on track by Monday."

Jake imagined running a hand up her thighs to the warmth he knew lay between them. "That's great."

Shay cocked her head as she looked at him. "Shouldn't you be in bed? You have to go to work in a few hours."

Jake let his head roll from side to side against the back of the chair. "Nope. If I go to sleep, you'll sneak off and do something you shouldn't be doing."

"I'm waiting for a call back from Ray or Chase to tell me they received the code. After that, I'm through for the day."

Jake sat up in his chair. "I'll go to sleep if you come with me." The words were out before he could stop them. But since they were out there...

"You are sleepy." Shay laughed, rose from the couch and offered him a hand. Having resolved so many problems had left her in a cheerful mood. "Here. Let me help you to your room."

Jake took her hand and, though he didn't need it, used her strength to lift himself out of the chair. His limbs were light as air now, his mind drugged with lust. Cleo had said to make Shay deal with his feelings. Right now he was feeling a lot.

When he failed to release her hand, Shay gave him a questioning look. "What're you doing, Jake?"

Pulling Shay against him, Jake buried his face in the crook of her neck. "You smell good," he said, nuzzling her soft, powder-smelling skin.

"You're tickling me." Shay laughed nervously and pushed at his chest.

"Am I?" he asked. Jake moved a hand to her bottom and pressed his hips against hers. She needed to understand he meant to do more than tickle her. He kissed her neck once, twice...reveling in the feel of her warm skin under his mouth.

The third kiss elicited a moan from Shay and she laid her head to the side. She was giving in much easier than he'd anticipated. Jake didn't waste any time wondering if this was the right thing to do. This time, he'd satisfy the hunger that had built up to volcanic levels.

He ran his hands down the coarse material of her skirt and, finger-by-finger, lifted her skirt to the curve of her bottom. Clutching the wool in one hand, he quickly moved his other to her round cheeks, hoping for black lace. To Jake's surprise, he found a satin lining still impeding his progress. "What is this, a trick skirt?" he chuckled, releasing the wool so both his hands could enjoy the slick material.

Shay captured his hands under her own. Her eyes were dark with lust and a little bit of fear.

It confused Jake. "What's wrong, Shay-Shay?" he asked gently.

"You haven't called me that since were kids."

"You're avoiding my question."

"Are you sure you want to do this?" she asked.

Jake pressed himself further against her. "What do you think?" he asked.

She didn't crack a smile. "That's not what I meant."

"I know." Jake knew she needed to hear that this would be more than a ten-years-without-a-woman thing. "I've wanted this since the moment I stepped foot in this apartment...maybe even longer. I promise I won't hurt you."

"You won't mean to. But I think you will, Jake." Her voice trembled, but she didn't move away.

"No." Jake moved his hands to her cheeks and kissed her lips tenderly. They were soft, moist and so much sweeter than he'd expected. "I love you, Shay-Shay," he whispered.

Shay gave in to his kiss. It hit her deep and low. Its power sent her head swimming for the second time that day. But this time there was no pain, no tiger claws ripping her in two. Only Jake and his wonderful hands that made her body tingle wherever they touched. And his wonderful mouth that knew just how to kiss her.

He drew back and Shay instantly missed his connection.

His mouth still wet from her kiss he said, "I've had a crush on you since middle school, you know."

"Have you?" Shay was surprised. Secretly she'd always loved Jake and Jerome, had spent every moment she could with them. "I was so scrawny and goofy-looking back then."

"I liked your wild hair." Jake pushed his fingers into her mass of curls. "I liked that you used to spout a fountain of profanities when Jerome and I yelled 'Shay-Shay Bay-Bay' down the hallway at school." His nimble fingers traveled down the rise of her breasts to her blouse and slowly began to undo the remaining buttons one by one.

"I wasn't really mad that you called me that," Shay confessed, enjoying the feel of his knuckles sliding down her torso.

"No?" He pushed her blouse away from her shoulders and kissed her along the line of her bra.

When his tongue slid soft and wet against her skin, Shay

nearly lost her mind. Closing her eyes against the feeling, she rolled her head back, helpless against the sensation.

"Uh…no," she finally managed to reply. It was getting harder to breathe. "I actually liked it."

"We knew you liked it." Jake moved his hands to cover her breasts. His thumbs circled the center of her satin bra. Her nipples budded under his touch, sending bolts of desire straight to the center of her. "Oh my God, Jake." She gripped his shoulders to keep from falling.

Finding the clasp, Jake released her bra and slid the straps down her arms. He stared at her as if he'd never seen breasts before. It occurred to her then, that it had been a long time for him. Of course, it had nearly been as long for her, too.

Jake's movements were no longer slow and relaxed. His hands trembled as he reached around her to unzip her skirt. Impatiently, he pushed the wool skirt and her panties down to her knees and from there they fell to the floor on their own. Shay stepped out of them and waited.

Jake stood there, not moving.

Shay grew warm under his gaze, fighting the impulse to cover herself.

Jake circled her slowly.

Unable to take the discomfort of standing there before him

naked, Shay crossed her arms over her breasts. "Why are you staring at me?" she demanded, wanting to pull her panties back up.

Coming to rest in front of her once more, Jake took her arms and unwrapped them from her breasts. "Because you're the most beautiful thing I've ever seen." His eyes were sincere as he spoke. "And if this is a dream, I want to remember every detail when I wake up."

It took a moment for the compliment to digest. Shay wasn't accustomed to receiving them. She decided turnabout was fair play. "What if it's me who's dreaming?"

A smile as wide as an ocean spread across his buttery brown face. His dimples looked deeper beneath the dark stubble covering his cheeks and jaw. He spread his arms wide as if to say, "Come and get me."

Shyness and discomfort melted away. It was Shay's turn to smile as she pulled his shirt over his head and let it drop to the floor. His muscles bunched delightfully when he moved. His chest was covered with hair that traveled down the hard lines of his stomach and disappeared into the top of his jeans.

"Need some help?" he teased.

Shay held her hand up. "I got this." Unzipping his pants, she slid her hands against the hard edges of his narrow hips and pushed his pants and briefs down together. It was like unwrapping a much-anticipated Christmas gift.

Jake stepped out of his clothes and turned slowly to allow her to savor every angle of his incredible physique. "Do I pass muster?" he asked.

"Oh, yeah," Shay said a little breathlessly, her eyes resting on his magnificent erection.

"You sure? You look a little—"

"I just hope it fits," she replied honestly. It had been a long time since she'd slept with a man, but she didn't recall the last one being quite so large.

Jake walked over to her and pulled her into his arms once again. "Something tells me it'll be just right." He kissed her forehead and just held her for a long moment.

Shay ran her fingers over the coarse fur of his chest. She loved the way he felt. Loved the way he smelled…so much like Jerome. She kissed his chest. Found his nipples and let her tongue roll around them until they hardened. Finally, she caressed the hard length of him, growing heated as he bucked and jerked under her touch.

"Let's go." Shay took his hand and led him to her bedroom. He followed like a willing slave.

Shay found herself shaking as if it were the first time. Of

course, according to Cleo, it would be. Her friend claimed that if you didn't get any for five years, technically you reverted back to being a virgin.

Thinking of her friend and how she was now betraying her troubled Shay for a moment. But then again, it was Cleo who was always telling her to go after what she wanted. She lay on the bed, watching Jake as he moved to straddle her. It was too late now to stop. Her body was craving the man like a drug.

His fingers entered her and sent her spiraling like nothing she'd ever felt. Massaging, teasing, tugging, circling all of her sensitive spots, Jake moved her to the edge of ecstasy. When she reached the precipice, time stood still. Shay arched upward, arms spread wide as her body exploded with white light. Cries of unspoken desires passed through her mouth, releasing her inhibitions, releasing embarrassment, releasing all of her.

Slowly, the light receded. Shay listened to her heart pounding in her ears, to her own panting breaths, feeling light as air. Jake spread her legs wider with his own then reared up on his knees. From out of nowhere, he produced a condom, unwrapped it and rolled it on.

Shay was no longer afraid. It was like a dream watching

such a divinely made man prepare to love her. A dream so sensual it warmed her fingertips and sent a rush to her head. She relaxed her legs and delighted in the feeling as he pushed his healthy length inside her weeping walls. His movements were strong, slow and deliberate. Shay didn't want the moment to end.

Jake moaned as he settled on top of her. "What'd I tell ya?"

Shay knew just what he meant. "I think it fits juuust right," she acknowledged languidly.

He moved his mouth to hers and let the roll of his tongue match the sensuous rhythm of his hips.

Unbelievably, Shay felt desire growing within her once again. She moved her hands over his smooth back and pushed them down to his hips. Even the man's buttocks were hard with muscles. She left her hands there and helped guide his movements as she pushed against him.

Jake abandoned Shay's mouth as his need overcame him. She felt too good, too tight, and too sweet for him to hold back any longer.

Her hips pushed against his and he pumped harder and faster. Her hands dug into the skin on his bottom, driving him insane. "Oh, Shay. Oh, Shay," he chanted, feeling all control leave him.

His body moved on its own, slave to some primal rhythm passed along through the ages. The dance was fast, virulent and chaotic. It seemed that every muscle, every cell in his body spun feverishly to center all of his energy in one place. Shay accepted his energy, seemed to coax it to ever spiraling madness.

Jake was helpless when the rhythm stopped. His muscles seized and energy and life burst from him in a long, wonderful climax. Beneath him, he could feel Shay tense as she screamed her pleasure once more. "Oh, Jerome," she sighed.

"Jerome?" Jake felt as if he'd received a physical blow. His elation burst like an over-filled balloon. He rolled from her quickly.

"Did I say that?" she asked innocently. "I meant Jake."

"You said Jerome." Jake was hurt beyond reason. He'd believed Cleo when she'd told him Shay hadn't been in love with his brother. Believed that Shay might one day love him. But now...

Shay sat up. "Don't be mad, Jake. I didn't mean it."

Jake hit the hallway just as Cleo came bursting through the front door.

"Hey, ya'll!" she yelled, then stopped when she caught sight of Jake standing in the hallway wearing absolutely nothing.

Jake cursed because he couldn't cry and stormed into his room and slammed the door.

Chapter Eleven

It certainly wasn't the first time Cleo had seen a man naked, but Jake Masters had been beyond magnificent as he stood framed in the arch of the hallway. Jake was now gone, but the image lived deliciously on.

Cleo sat on the couch arm to take a moment to collect her breath and her thoughts. "Thank you, Lord, for your kindness and mercy," she whispered.

It was then that she noticed the piles of clothes on the floor. And hadn't Jake been coming from Shay's room before he stormed into his own? Two and two came together in Cleo's head with a ringing of bells. Shay had finally gotten laid!

Instead of the quiet content of sexual satisfaction however, Jake had worn the face of an angered male beast. Whatever was wrong, she wasn't going to find out about it hanging out in the living room. Cleo tossed Shay's coat, purse, boots and hat that she'd retrieved from the office onto the couch and raced to Shay's bedroom on tiptoe.

Her door was wide open. It was dark in the room, but she could see Shay lying on the bed with a sheet pulled over her head.

Cleo closed the door and moved to sit beside her friend on the bed. "Shay?" She tried to pull down the sheet, but Shay clung to it tightly. "Come on, girl. Tell me what happened. I've never seen a man so pissed in my life."

Only sniffles came from the other side of the sheet.

"You crying?" Cleo couldn't believe it. Her friend was always in control. "Tell me what happened, Shay. It couldn't be that bad."

"Yes it could," came Shay's morose reply.

The suspense was making Cleo jumpy. "What was it? He couldn't perform? You couldn't perform? What?"

"It was great, Cleo." She brought the sheet down to her chin. Tears spilled from her eyes as she spoke. "I've never felt anything like that before."

"Now you're making me jealous." Cleo dropped her shoes on the floor and folded her legs on the bed. "But if it was all that, why're both of you in such a mood?"

Her eyes squeezed shut. "I called him Jerome." She barely squeaked out the words.

"Great day in the morning!" Cleo couldn't keep her mouth

from hanging open. "You didn't."

"I did."

Cleo had known enough men in her life to know calling one of them by the name of another didn't score any points. And Jake... She recalled how hopeful he'd looked after she told him that Shay hadn't been in love with his brother. He wouldn't trust another word she said.

"What should I do?" Shay asked.

"Leave him alone." Cleo shrugged.

"What? Why?" Shay sat up, careful to keep the sheet wrapped around her torso. "I need to make it up to him."

Cleo shook her head and sighed. "This isn't the kind of thing you can make up, Shay. The brother's got to get over it."

"How's he going to get over it if I don't prove to him that it's him I love and not Jerome?"

She said it with such conviction that Cleo perked up. "You love him?" she asked. "You sure?"

"Yeah," she said cautiously. "But you do, too, don't you?"

"Me? No." Cleo waved away the thought. "I think the man is fine and all, but he's not my type."

"But you and he were trying to get together, weren't you?"

Not at all surprised that Shay had paid such close attention to the goings on around her, Cleo decided to come clean. "We did meet in secret. But it was to talk about you."

"Me?"

"Yeah. We're both worried about you."

"Why?"

Now Cleo was angry. "Because you hold everything in so tight it gives you an anxiety attack. Because even when you land in the hospital, you don't think anything of it. Because you won't let anybody help you. That's why!"

"I don't need any help, Cleo," Shay shot back. "I had no father when I was a kid. At the age of nine I was taking care of my drunken mother. I made something of myself, Cleo, and I did it with no one's help but my own."

"That's right, you did." Cleo jumped off the bed and found her shoes. "But that doesn't mean you don't need anybody. Why do you think you called him Jerome?" she challenged, pointing toward the door.

"I don't know. Maybe I'm still in love with Jerome."

"You just said you were in love with Jake."

Shay groaned. "I've had this problem since we were kids," she admitted.

"What problem?" Cleo's curiosity temporarily subdued her anger.

"I've been in love with both Jake and Jerome since I can remember." She folded her arms around her legs as she spoke. "I loved Jerome because he was popular and charming. He was king of the basketball court and all the girls swooned over him. Jake was quieter, more studious. We used to talk 'til all hours of the night whenever I went over to study with him. He kept geometry from kicking my butt. Seemed I was most in love with whoever was in the room with me at the time. I'm doing the same thing now."

"Well then, girl, you've got serious issues." Cleo shook her head. "No man wants to think he came in second to any other man."

"How can he be threatened when Jerome's not even..." Shay's voice broke. "When he's not around?"

"He's in your head," Cleo insisted. "He's in your heart." She put a hand on Shay's bare shoulder. "Now you've brought him to your bed. Shay, somehow you've got to prove to Jake that he's the one you love. Just like you'd have to do if Jerome were still here."

"That's impossible, Cleo. How do I choose?"

"Maybe you only really love Jake. Maybe you were just in love with the idea of loving Jerome."

"Now you're talking crazy, Cleo. Of course, I loved Jerome.

You saw how tore up I was when he brought his women friends home."

"Humph." Cleo put a fist to her hip. "Not enough to challenge his behind on it."

"Don't start that again." Shay's tone turned irritable.

"All I know is you look at Jake a lot differently than you did Jerome—"

"Oh. And that proves everything." Shay threw up a hand. "I knew this was a bad idea." Shay wrapped the sheet around her in short, angry movements and left the bed. "I should've never let Jake stay here. Get out of my way, Cleo. I need a drink."

Cleo didn't move. "You need to leave that wine alone. There are better ways to deal with your problems."

Though it was dark, Cleo could feel the heat coming from Shay's eyes. "I'm a grown woman, Cleopatra Roberts. I'll drink what and when I want."

The urge to wring her friend's neck was powerfully strong, but some divine restraint kept Cleo's arms folded tightly against her chest. "You're only hurting yourself, you know?"

"Since when is that a crime?" Shay shot back.

"It's not a crime. It's a damned shame." Cleo gripped the doorknob tightly and swung the door open. "I love you,

Shay. But you're pissing me off right now, so I'm going."

"Fine. Go." Shay followed her into the hallway. "I don't need you or your bad advice."

Cleo was wounded and angered by the venom in Shay's tone. "You don't mean that."

"I meant it. And I think you're happy that this happened. You wanted to add Jake to your long list of male conquests, didn't you? You're mad 'cause I got him first."

"You think this is a contest?" Cleo couldn't believe what she was hearing. "How can you even form your lips—"

"Because I know you, Cleo. I know you and Jerome had an affair." Her breaths were coming in short bursts now. "I know even though you both tried to hide it from me."

Struck dumb by the true statement, Cleo could only stand there with her mouth hanging open.

"Oh, so the always witty Cleopatra Roberts suddenly has nothing to say." Shay's voice was laced with acidic hatred. "I didn't look at Jerome the way a woman in love should. Is that what you told yourself, Cleo? Did that make it all right to creep around with him at night, then pretend to console me the next day?"

"You don't understand..." It was Cleo's turn to have her voice break with emotion. "I loved Jerome, but I didn't want to hurt you. We broke it off because of you."

"Spare me. It ended because, like all the others, Jerome got tired of you."

"That's a horrible thing to say." Cleo's heart was shattering. It had been painful enough to deny herself the one man she'd ever loved because of her friendship with Shay. It was excruciating to have that same friend trivialize her feelings.

"Do you ever wonder why I'm your only friend? Why the people at the office talk about you behind your back?" Cleo now wanted to offer hurt for hurt. "It's because you make it so hard to love you, Shay. You have this prickly wall around you that no one can get through. You're so lonely that you thought the only man who was kind to you was in love with you. Jerome loved me. Make no mistake about it."

"You, my only friend, tried to take the thing that meant the most to me. How many more friends do I need like that?"

"What means the most to you is you, Shay Bennett. I didn't see a single tear leave your eye at Jerome's wake. If he meant so much to you, why weren't you crying?"

Shay swallowed hard before answering. "I cried afterward, but hated myself for it. Tears are weak. They don't do anything to honor a person who passes."

"They show that your heart was touched by them, Shay.

Don't you know that?" Cleo looked toward Jake's closed door. Her heart went out to him. "I hope Jake leaves here tomorrow 'cause your behind doesn't deserve him."

Before Shay could say anything else, Cleo was across the living room and out the front door. Hot tears streamed as she made her way to the elevator.

Wait! Stop! I didn't mean it, Shay wanted to shout, but pride and anger kept the words from leaving her lips.

The front door had slammed soundly shut. Cleo was gone and Shay knew she would never be back.

Pushing her fingers into the soft depths of her hair, Shay massaged her scalp in frustration as she blew out a long breath. The sheet she'd kept wrapped around her dropped to the floor without ceremony. Stepping out of it, Shay made her way to the kitchen. Maybe, if she had enough wine, she could convince herself that she really didn't care that she'd just chased away her best friend.

Chapter Twelve

Angry winds bit at Jake's nose and eyes, which remained uncovered despite his efforts to bundle up against the subzero temperature. It was only a few blocks to the subway, but walking against the hawking winds made it take far longer than usual this evening.

Relief came as he took the steps down into the station. Removing his muffler from his mouth, he took a deep breath. It wasn't exactly warm inside, but at least there was protection from the biting gusts outside. Jake pulled off a glove with his teeth and fished his token from his pocket to drop into the metal receptacle. He moved to the platform and stomped feeling back into his feet as he waited for his train to work.

For the past few days he'd felt less and less lucky to be free from prison. He'd so looked forward to repairing the relationships with his family, to starting his life over again and to finding closure with Charlotte White.

Shay, of course, he hadn't counted on. He was mad for her,

even now. Especially now. He wished he'd never kissed her, never made love to her, because it took all his strength not to creep into her room every night and fill his senses with the drug of her love. He'd almost convinced himself that he didn't care if she thought about Jerome while he made love to her. But it did matter. It mattered a lot.

Things were very different now. He and Shay hadn't said two words to each other the entire weekend and Cleo hadn't stepped foot inside the apartment. Given her hallway argument with Shay, Jake couldn't blame her a bit. Jerome and Cleo. Shit. She must've been the woman with "complications" surrounding her that Jerome had spoken of the last time he'd visited the prison. It was too bad. They would've been perfect together.

It was all too much drama, Jake decided. "Too much drama," he said aloud to no one.

"I beg your pardon?" an older woman standing nearby asked. She was short and wore a bright red scarf wrapped around her head and neck.

"Nothing," Jake replied. "Talking to myself."

"Oh." The woman nodded and turned her attention back to the rails. After a moment, she turned back to Jake. "What's your name?" she asked.

"Me? Jake Masters, ma'am," he answered politely, wondering why it mattered to her.

"Your mama Olivia Masters?"

A little surprised Jake replied, "Yeah. Do you know her?"

The old woman nodded. "Go to church with her every Sunday. I'm Pruda Daniels. I saw your brother with your mama all the time. That's how I know'd ya. You was the one in jail, 's that right?"

Jake looked around anxiously. It wasn't something he wanted everyone to hear. "Yes, ma'am."

She reached over and patted his arm. "It wasn't right what happened to you, boy. Wasn't right."

"Thank you, Miss Daniels." Curiosity rose then. Maybe his mother was ill and that was why she hadn't answered the door when he'd visited her a few months ago. "How is my mother, Miss Daniels?"

"Not good, boy. Not good. She prays for forgiveness that don't never come. It's eatin' at her somethin' fierce."

"Forgiveness for what?" Jake asked.

The woman peered at him with lively brown eyes. "That ain't for me to say."

Jake nodded his understanding.

Pruda looked back toward the tracks.

Jake could see a train coming down the tunnel. "It was nice meeting you, Miss Daniels. This is my train."

"Nice meeting you, too. Stop by and see your mama sometime. Come to church. Trinity Baptist," she offered.

Jake simply nodded, not wanting to make promises he wouldn't keep. He hopped into the warmth of the subway car and looked back toward the platform. Miss Pruda Daniels had gotten lost in the thickening crowd.

Twenty minutes later, Jake arrived at the call center. Before he could remove his boots and toss his coat over a chair, Lela was in his office. "Got some news for ya," she said, filling the doorway with her presence. Her hair was no longer gray and spiky, but the neon red of a home dye job gone bad.

"Good or bad?" Jake asked, dropping into his chair.

"Depends." Lela sat in the chair opposite the desk from him. "The brass is lookin' at expanding the call center. They want a hundred new reps in here by May."

"That's only two months from now." Surprise sprang Jake from his leisurely recline. "Are they going to be spread among the shifts? Where are we going to put them?"

Lela started to laugh. "I told 'em you'd be the right one to give the project to. You like all that analysis crap."

Jake was confused. "What're you talking about, Lela?"

"Makin' you to project manager, Jake. You need to help me hire a section manager or two to replace you, come to a few meetings later this week and figure out how we're going to make this expansion work."

"Are you sure about this?" Jake asked.

"Positive." Lela rose and headed out the door. "By the way," she turned around, "did I mention there'll be a substantial raise in pay?"

Jake smiled. "You're the best."

"Naw." Lela shook her fierce red mane. "You're a waste of talent on the night shift. We need to get you some exposure. Take the night off and put Donald in charge. I need you here at eight tomorrow morning to knock the brass off their flabby behinds."

She was gone and Jake was stupefied. Maybe he had achieved one of his goals, after all. With a "substantial" pay increase he might be able to move out of Shay's apartment. He refused to be Jerome's replacement.

She said she loved me. Jake's heart wanted to hold on. She said she beat Cleo to you. His mind forced reason into his internal conversation. No matter how he looked at it, Shay had used him the night they were together. An old tune played in his mind. Like Hootie and the Blowfish, he wanted to keep on being used until Shay used him up. He hummed the song wistfully, feeling more whipped than a dog.

"Hey, boss." It was Donald standing in his doorway. "Got a customer complaint on 41. You wanna talk with her?"

"Sure," Jake said, happy that soon he'd be out of the customer service business. Most of the time, he made the customers happy, but it had become wearing. "But I'm leaving after this one. Can you handle the floor?"

"What's it worth to you?" Donald teased.

"How about a promotion to section manager?" Jake asked in all seriousness.

"You mean it?" His eyes sparkled like blue diamonds.

"I'll work on it." Jake pressed the appropriate extension as Donald nearly danced toward the maze of cubicles. "Thank you for holding. This is Jake, how may I help you?"

"Jake? Jake Masters?" The woman on the other end of the line was crying.

"Who is this?"

"It's…Charlotte."

Jake covered the phone and groaned. What could the woman possibly want? "I didn't give you this number,

Charlotte."

"I know. I...I need your help, Jake."

"With what?"

Muffled sobs came across the line.

Jake was growing concerned. "What is it, Charlotte? Are you hurt?"

"I need you to come get me, Jake."

"Where's your husband? Why don't you call him?" The last time he'd helped her out, he'd landed in jail. Jake wasn't about to fall for the same trick twice.

"He's going to kill me. He's going...to kill me." Her sobs grew louder.

"What happened? He catch you in bed with your latest conquest?" Jake couldn't blame the man for reaching his limit. "You have family, don't you?"

"They won't help me anymore. No one will. Please, Jake. Please."

"Where are you?" Jake asked, knowing it was a mistake.

He scribbled down the address she gave, noting it was located just down the street. "Tell you what, I'll think about it. But if I'm not there in fifteen minutes, don't wait around for me." Jake hung up before she could beg further. It went against his nature to turn away from anyone in need, but it took Jake exactly five minutes to decide what to do about Charlotte White.

❖

The tiger was back. It had crept up on Shay slowly since her falling out with Cleo. It had grown stronger each day, as she and Jake had given one another the cold shoulder. It had been a wicked day at work trying to farm out Sydney's work before she left. Her last day was this coming Friday and Shay had been totally unsuccessful in convincing the woman to stay.

Shay lay in bed in the dark, letting the sharp claws of the tiger rip her insides to shreds as recent memories deepened each wound. "The thing that means most to you is you," Cleo had accused. She was right, Shay realized.

Everything...all she did...was for the sake of self-preservation. She hadn't let Jerome know how she felt for fear of certain rejection. He'd wanted to be with Cleo. Shay had known it, but couldn't accept it. She'd made it impossible for either of them to explore the relationship without feeling guilty about hurting her feelings.

Only now did Shay realize that her grief for Jerome was

mostly due to guilt. His death meant that her wrong could never be righted. She was wicked and self-centered and deserved to die. Fresh shards of pain ripped through her chest as if to do her bidding.

Throwing aside her covers, Shay struggled into a pair of jeans and a T-shirt. She had to leave the apartment. The memories were growing too vivid, her conscience too heavy. Covering her hair with a baseball cap, she started toward the living room only to be stopped cold by a violent wave of dizziness.

"Oh no. Not again." Grasping for the arm of the chair, Shay eased herself to the floor. Sucking in a huge breath, she tried to keep darkness at bay. Her mouth turned dry and her body felt hot as a desert as the tiger's claws seared her chest once more.

It was too much. Shay stopped fighting and acquiesced to the pain. Lying spread-eagled on the floor, finally, she cried. She cried for the loss of Jerome, for her manipulation of Cleo, for causing Jake pain. She'd lost everyone who had ever meant anything to her and she didn't care anymore if she lived or died.

Jake pushed his way inside quickly. The cries he'd heard only moments before had quieted to heart-breaking whimpers. He found Shay on the floor next to the chair, her face wet with tears and her hair long ago sprung loose of the cap that lay nearby. "Shay? What happened?" he asked, not knowing whether to touch her.

Her eyes remained tightly closed as Shay rolled her head miserably from side-to-side. "I'm sorry, Jake. So sorry."

"Sorry about what?" Jake was relieved that she knew who he was. He placed a hand to her face and wiped the wet from her cheek. "Why are you on the floor?"

Opening her eyes only a sliver, she looked at him. "Cleo's right. I don't deserve..." Instead of finishing her thought, Shay closed her eyes once again and wiped her face roughly with both hands. "I slipped. I'll be fine."

Jake helped her to her feet. He knew she was lying about why she was on the floor and grew angry. "Did you have another attack? It wouldn't be the worst thing in the world to ask for help sometimes, Shay."

"Should I take a number, then?" Shay was looking past Jake to the open door.

Jake turned to see Charlotte standing in the doorway. "What are you doing here?"

It relieved Shay a bit to see his shock.

"I know you don't want to see me, but I had to talk to you."

Jake muttered an obscenity just low enough that Shay couldn't discern it. He arced his arm from Charlotte to Shay and then back to the woman standing in the doorway. "Shay, this is—"

"I know who she is, Jake." Shay shot him a sobering look.

Charlotte took a step inside the apartment. "I was wondering if I could talk to you in private for just a moment, Jake."

Jake sighed and pulled the hat from his head. He walked behind Charlotte to close the door. "Have a seat," he offered half-heartedly.

Shay could feel herself growing angry. This woman was up to no good, she was sure of it. She walked to the kitchen to get a drink of water. "Would either of you like something while I'm in the kitchen?" she offered.

Charlotte shook her head and shot Shay a cross look.

Shay lifted an eyebrow and glared at the woman sitting on her couch in her apartment, hoping she understood that Jake Masters was not on her to-do list tonight.

They talked low enough that Shay couldn't hear them as she first poured, then drank a glass of ice water. The little bit of pain left from her panic attack retreated, giving Shay an opportunity to focus completely on the drama unfolding before her.

Charlotte's face contorted with fear, then sadness as she twisted tissue in her expensively manicured hands.

Shay moved around the kitchen, removing pots and pans as if preparing to cook dinner. She shook her head as she watched Jake's irritation turn to compassion. It had taken Charlotte White exactly two minutes to have the man agreeing to whatever request she'd made.

Jake rose from the seat beside the woman and headed for his bedroom.

Shay made sure he didn't miss her questioning look.

He cleared his throat and spoke in a low voice. "Charlotte just needs some cash to get her to her sister's house in Washington D.C. She's having a little trouble at home," he added with a whisper. "I'll be right back with that money for you," he tossed over his shoulder to Charlotte.

"Thanks, Jake," She answered with a sniffle.

Jake could feel Shay's disapproval following him until he turned the corner. He'd decided to help Charlotte, not because he believed a word of what she'd said, or because of how pitiful she looked, but because it seemed easier to get her out of town than to risk running into her everywhere he went. "You can call a cab now if you like," he yelled from his bedroom.

He could hear Shay strike up a conversation with Charlotte while he was out of the room. It occurred to him that she was using the tone she'd used to sweet-talk the guy from Blue Banana out of his code secrets. Jake wondered what she was up to as he rummaged through his top drawer to find his "stash." Buying Charlotte an airline ticket to D.C. was going to wipe out his fledgling emergency funds. Even flying standby cost a mint these days. Hopefully it would be money well spent.

When he returned to the living room, the women seemed to be involved in casual chitchat, but there was an undercurrent a weird vibe that set the room on edge.

"Were you able to get a cab?" Jake asked Charlotte hopefully.

"Oh, no. Got sidetracked." She cut her eyes slightly at Shay and moved toward the phone.

Jake sent a questioning look to his roommate.

Shay shrugged as if to say, "I'm completely innocent."

Jake knew better.

Charlotte finished her call. "They said a cab would be here in fifteen minutes. Look, Jake," Charlotte moved up close beside him and lowered her voice, "You've been great, but

I've been thinking about this. I don't think it would be right to go to D.C. Just give me the cab fare and I'll pay you back as soon as I can."

"Are you sure? What about your husband?"

Charlotte looked tired as she waved away the thought. "I'll be okay. I've lived through it this long."

Shay made a sound from the other side of the room.

"You don't need me in your way," Charlotte added with a little attitude. "Looks like you've got your hands full already." She wasn't looking at Shay, but it was clear whom the comment was directed toward. "Why don't we go down-stairs and wait," Charlotte suggested.

"I'll come with you," Shay said, grabbing her coat.

Jake re-buttoned his own coat and tried to figure out what was up with Shay. Was she suddenly jealous of him? Was that why she was having a pissing contest with Charlotte? He had to admit the thought had a certain nurturing effect on his wounded ego.

The three of them took the elevator down to the apartment lobby. They waited just inside the doors, Charlotte on the right, Jake on the left and Shay wedged between them in the narrow space. Whatever game she was playing, Jake was starting to enjoy it. They waited in silence. When the cab finally arrived, Charlotte looked back at Jake as if she had something to say. She seemed to think better of it after glancing at Shay. "Bye, Jake," she finally said. "Thanks for your help."

Jake waved, happy to be rid of her. "Wanna tell me what that was all about?" he asked Shay a little smugly as the cab slid away into the night.

Shay looked at him and sighed. "You are so clueless sometimes, Jake. Why do you think she called you tonight?"

Jake shrugged and followed Shay back to the elevator. "She was having a rough night. She had an argument with her husband and he was starting to get violent."

"Why didn't she call 911?" Shay entered the elevator. Jake followed.

"She said he's a lawyer. No one ever believes her when she says he hits her."

"Does she have bruises or anything?"

"She says he hits her in the gut and it takes a while for bruises to form."

"And you believed that?" Shay shook her head.

"Well...Sorta," Jake admitted.

Shay laughed. "It's a good thing I was here to save you this time, then."

Amused, Jake followed her from the elevator to their apartment. "Oh so you saved me?"

"Yes, I did," she affirmed once they got inside. "That woman was about to use you for something. I wasn't able to find out exactly what, but I made it clear to her that she wasn't getting away with it."

Charlotte had been up to something. That was probably why Jake's radar had been up all evening. But he figured he could handle whatever it was. He'd made a point not to touch her just in case she decided to accuse him of rape again. "I'll have you to know that I had that situation under control," Jake said.

"Just like the night that landed you in jail?" Shay said with a laugh. "That woman schemes on a level I've never seen before."

"Turns out it wasn't her doing the scheming," Jake confessed as he removed his coat. "It was her husband. I had to take the fall for the rape so her pimp could avoid going to jail and her lawyer husband could buy her freedom."

A light had reached Shay's eyes that Jake hadn't seen for a long time. "You're making that up," she accused, playfully dropping onto the couch.

"I'm not. That's what Charlotte told me when I ran into

her the other day." Jake didn't go into more detail about who he was with the first time he'd spoken with Charlotte. It was too soon to speak of Cleo.

"And you believe that?" Shay was incredulous. "Oh Jake, you poor, trusting, kind-hearted soul."

"She's a spoiled kid, Shay, who's always done what other people have told her to do. I know it sounds like a soap opera. Maybe it's time, maybe not. Regardless, there's no good reason for sending an innocent man to jail."

"You're right about that," Shay admitted quietly. "There's no good reason for what a lot of people do."

The light had left her eyes and Jake found himself missing it. "What are you thinking?" he asked gently.

She shook her head slowly.

"Don't tell me you don't want to talk about it." Jake moved to sit beside her on the couch. "You've got to open up to somebody or you're going to tear yourself apart."

"I can't." Shay looked up at him as misery swam in her eyes. "I'm too ashamed."

"Try me," he offered.

"And you're too forgiving," she whispered. "You just gave cash to a woman who sent you to jail for ten years because you felt sorry for her."

"Actually, it was to get rid of her," Jake confessed.

"You did feel sorry for her, didn't you?"

He nodded. "Is that so wrong?" He wasn't sure if he was asking her or himself

"I wish I was more like you, Jake." She swallowed hard before she spoke again. "I wish I thought about other people more than myself. Here you are, the one person who should be angrier at the world than anyone I know, yet ready to offer me comfort because I'm feeling sorry for myself and making myself sick. That takes a hell of a lot of character, Jake."

Humbled by her words, Jake didn't know what to say.

"I need to find a way to forgive myself for my past sins before I'll let you have a go at it. Okay?"

"Okay," Jake agreed because he wasn't sure what else to do. "Wanna go to church with me Sunday?" he asked suddenly, remembering Pruda Daniels invitation.

"What?"

"You may find some answers at church. Besides, I might get a chance to see my mother and...I don't want to go by myself in case she avoids me again. Would you come with me?"

Shay smiled. "Sure."

"Oh, by the way," Jake stood up, feeling better than he had in days, "I got a new job at work. Lela says there'll be a significant increase in pay. Want to join me in a toast?" he asked, heading for the kitchen.

"Uh…only if it's a soda, Jake." Shay looked a little funny. "That Merlot's been giving me a headache lately."

Secretly, Jake was relieved. It looked like Shay was trying to make some changes. He was glad. "Soda it is," he said.

Jake poured Coke over ice in two glasses. He delivered Shay's drink to her on the couch. "Toast?" he offered.

"To what?" Shay smiled sadly. "Your wicked roommate?"

Lowering his glass, Jake took her hand in his own, brought it to his lips and gently kissed it. "You just take everything way too seriously."

"I don't know any other way to take things, Jake." She poked at the ice in her glass and sucked the soda from her finger. "How much of Cleo's and my conversation did you hear the other night?" she asked tentatively.

Jake settled back on the couch and focused on his own drink before answering. "Enough to know you slept with me to keep Cleo from doing it."

Shay shook her head. "I know that's what it sounded like Jake, but I want you to know that I slept with you because

I...I...you know."

"I don't know, Shay." Jake's eyes were now riveted on the woman he loved. Hope sprang up within him. "Tell me." He wanted to hear what her true feelings were.

Shay turned to face him. Her eyes were troubled, her pale lips turned down. "My feelings for you are complicated," she began. "I think I'm in love with you, but I don't know if it's because you remind me of Jerome or..."

It wasn't the answer Jake wanted to hear. "Or what?"

"Or I'm just desperate to be loved." Her head dropped immediately and she seemed completely ashamed of what she'd just said.

Jake was floored. He could see just how hard it was for her to finally confess to him, to anyone, just how lonely she was. Finally, she'd let down her walls of defense. Don't blow it, Jake, he cautioned himself, knowing this would be his only chance to get inside her head.

Jake placed his glass of soda on the coffee table, took Shay's glass and did the same. He took her in his arms and kissed her as he'd never kissed a woman before. There were no words to describe how deeply he loved her, no ways to tell her how much he cherished being in her presence. Instead of words he used his kisses. Playful nips and pecks to help her understand that love could be fun and easy and light-hearted. Soft, gentle ones to tell her how much she touched his heart. Deep wet ones to explain the passion that burned hotter and brighter for her with every breath, with every touch.

When he finally finished all he had to explain to her, Jake pulled away, never letting his eyes leave her as she panted on the couch. "You're not a desperate woman, Shay Bennett," he said breathlessly. "Since I've known you, you've always gone after what you wanted. But if you're confused about your feelings for me, I just need you to know one thing."

Her eyes looked drugged as she watched him. "What's that, Jake?"

"I want you to love me for myself. I deserve your whole heart. And I deserve to know very soon if you'll ever be able to give that to me."

Shay shot up on the couch as Jake got up to walk away. "When's soon?" she asked, holding onto his arm.

"Before my heart breaks and I'm forced to settle for someone else." He headed for the door when she released him. He had to leave, before he tried to convince her further. "See you, later," he said, grabbing his coat and boots from the chair where he'd abandoned them earlier. He left her, hoping with all his heart that he'd just done the right thing.

Chapter Thirteen

Charlotte awoke at midnight, disappointed to find Damian lying next to her. She'd been high when they'd gone to bed last night, but despite the drugs, Charlotte had barely been able to take the man's touch.

She'd been dreaming of Jake. Dreaming that he'd completely forgiven her for putting him in jail and that he had made love to her. He had forgiven her, she decided. How could he not forgive her? The whole plan to frame him was Damian's, he was the one who deserved to be suffering right now, not her.

Charlotte felt bad for trying to trick Jake and wanted to make it up to him. She'd made up the story about running to her sister's house. Cherese, with her high-and-mighty attitude, was the last person on earth she wanted to visit. No matter how much money Charlotte flashed, her sister never gave her any respect.

All she'd wanted was to find a way to spend some time with Jake that night. She could've had him wrapped around her finger if it hadn't been for his roommate. Shay, was it? Witch. Had the nerve to tell her to stay away from Jake.

Charlotte had backed off, all right, but only to have time to think. She had a prison of her own to break out of and this time drugs and alcohol wouldn't be enough to free her. She needed something more permanent.

Damian rolled over and draped her waist with his arm. Charlotte tried to wiggle free, only to feel his fingers grip her soft flesh. "You awake?" he asked. A long hard-on pressed against her thigh and Charlotte knew the question was supposed to be foreplay.

"I'm not in the mood," she said irritably.

Damian kissed her arm. "I am."

Without the aid of pharmaceuticals, Charlotte couldn't keep her feelings below the surface. "I don't want you to touch me. Okay?" She threw his arm off and left the bed.

"Hold up." Damian propped himself up on pillows and watched her throw on a T-shirt and shorts. "You're my wife. This is your wifely duty

"Damian, I'm tired," Charlotte said. She made up her mind to tell him her true feelings. She'd had ten years of holding them in or covering them with the haze of drugs. Charlotte couldn't hold them in any longer. "I'm tired of pretending what we have is a marriage. This was a business deal. Nothing more."

He shifted slightly. "What are you saying, Charlotte? You thinking of leaving me?"

"Why do you care, Damian?" she asked hopefully. "You don't love me and I don't love you."

She could see the shadow of his arms across his narrow chest. "You just don't know what love is."

"What do you mean?" she asked, crossing her arms across her slightly chilled body.

"I know what you do the nights you come home late or not at all. I have every lie you've ever told etched in my mind."

His tone was soft and low; so full of emotion it scared Charlotte. She rubbed the goose bumps along the back of her neck.

"I've said nothing. I've suffered your indiscretions by telling myself I don't care if you sleep with other men," Damian said. "I deluded myself to the point where I believed my fondest wish was to come home one day and find you in the act. That way I could watch awhile and then jump right in." He gave a short, pained laugh. "I'm truly grateful you've never brought one of them home. If I knew another man had been here with you," he moved a hand lovingly across the sheets beside him, "I don't know what I would've done."

Charlotte sighed and sank to the edge of the bed. "Do you know why I sleep with other men, Damian?" she asked wearily. "It's the only time I get to have power. I get to choose who. I get to choose when. It's not you or Machete or my father telling me what to do.

"I do know what love is," she continued, "and I know I'll never find it if I stay here with you."

"What do you want, Charlotte?" he asked in frustration. "How much more do I have to give you?"

"Nothing!" Charlotte yelled. "Love isn't money. It isn't gold or diamonds or a new house with expensive furniture. Love is having a man take my hand because he loves the feel of it, not to possess it. It's having someone see me as a woman, not an adornment. We're not together because we dated and fell in love. We're together because you bought me. I want to be free. What will it take for me to be free from you, Damian?" she asked desperately.

Silence filled the dark spaces of the room. Damian's voice broke through the stillness. "I've always seen you as free to make your own choices. I thought you slept with other men because I didn't spend enough time with you. In spite of how we began, I wasn't trying to imprison you. Lord knows I've been afraid that you might exercise your right to walk out the door each and every day for the past ten years." In fact, I'm surprised you stayed so long."

Charlotte moved slowly across the room to the chair near the window. All this time she'd felt oppressed and she could have simply walked out the door? What had really been keeping her here? Charlotte thought hard about the question. She concluded that the answer was fear. As much as she desired independence, she was afraid to be alone. She'd thought to leave Damian by running to Jake. With sudden insight she realized that simply trading one man for another wouldn't have solved her problem.

"If you want to leave," Damian's voice choked, "I won't try to keep you. I can't stand you turning away from me any longer. I can't take it."

"And you don't deserve it," she admitted. It was her hatred for feeling trapped that had made his touch repulsive. Prior to their marriage she'd found him quite desirable. "I don't want to leave. Not yet. I don't even know where I'd go," she answered honestly. She didn't get along with her sister and her parents had long ago disowned her when she'd shown up high at one of their dinner parties.

"Then why don't you stay until you figure it out?" Damian

offered.

It was kind. It seemed the kindest thing Charlotte had ever heard. Squeezing her eyes shut forced warm tears down her face. The man had loved her for ten years and she'd treated him like crap. All she'd been able to see was her own needs, her own desires. "You don't owe me that," she said.

Damian was silent for long moments before he finally answered, "I know."

Because it was cold in the room, Charlotte walked back over to the bed and moved under the warm flannel sheets and heavy down comforter. This time, instead of turning her back on her husband, Charlotte moved to him and laid her head on his shoulder.

His hand moved over her hair in soothing strokes. Charlotte closed her eyes and found it surprising that his touch wasn't disgusting or revolting at all.

❂

It was Friday. Shay had been distracted all morning and had to be re-directed twice during their status meeting with Team Dynamics. In fact, she'd been rendered completely stupid since the moment Jake had kissed her the previous night.

She'd dreamed and daydreamed about the kiss over and over again. She closed her eyes and leaned back in her desk chair to play the memory once more.

"It's time for Sydney's retirement party," Mirna interrupted.

Embarrassed to have been caught, Shay sprang from her chair. "Already?"

"Yeah. What's the matter with you today?" Mirna asked. "Didn't sleep?"

Shay shook her head. Mega horny, she wanted to say. But she had to be professional with Mirna. Besides, she just wasn't Cleo who would've gotten a great laugh out of the comment. Shay missed her friend. "I'm fine," she lied.

Shay followed Mirna to the large conference room. Sydney's staff had done a great job of decorating. Balloons and streamers hung from the ceiling and resting in the middle of the conference table, a huge cake was decorated to show a cartoon computer with a message scrolled across its screen: "Programmers never retire. When they crash they get re-booted. We'll miss you, Sydney."

Still not happy about losing a good manager, Shay had somehow managed to re-organize the staff and keep testing on track while she met with the woman daily to work on other loose ends. It occurred to Shay that they had gotten along famously this past week and that it should've always been that way.

For the first time in a long time, Shay sat back and watched the interaction of her staff. She knew nearly nothing about any of them though she'd managed the technical group for close to four years. The things she knew about her managers had been gleaned from brief conversations she'd overheard rather than initiated.

Since childhood, she'd lived on the island of Shay. How much life had she missed out on simply because she'd refused to trust there was anything good in other people? She was Superwoman. Able to free herself from the shackles of a dysfunctional family and poverty. Able to achieve a vice presidency in only ten years. Able to die a lonely death at the age of thirty-six because of chronic anxiety attacks.

Was that really why she wanted to love Jake? Or was it because of the way he kissed her? As the memory brought warmth to her body and a smile to her lips, Shay struggled to remain at the party. She wanted to go home and wake him from his sleep and feel his arms wrap her tight as his kisses rendered her defenseless once again.

Shay became aware of a sudden shift in mood around her.

She focused her attention fully on the people at the front of the room. Chase Broward was now toasting Sydney with a lifted cup of punch. "Now y'all ain't gonna believe this. But I want ya to know that Sydney's group discovered why the new code Blue Banana gave us still wasn't working with the Team Dynamics software just last night. This mornin', just for you, darlin'," he spoke to Sydney, "my programmers were able to fix the damn coding and we're gonna' meet our deadline after all!"

Shay couldn't believe her ears. Her whoops of joy joined the others as a true celebration began.

Sydney shushed everyone and managed to quiet them down to say a few words. "I'd like to take credit for saving the project, but I have to confess, it wasn't my doing."

Shay stood in the back of the room, humbled by what she knew Sydney was about to say.

"In fact, our boss, Shay Bennett, has been running testing for the past two weeks. After she got most of the code from Blue Banana she's been working with my programmers to find the problems. It was Shay who actually cracked the code, so let's give her a hand."

The staff applauded and turned toward Shay, who acknowledged the compliment with a few thank yous and nods of her head. Deciding that she had more to say, Shay made her way to the front. Chase bowed gallantly and moved aside to stand next to Ray.

"Thank you, Sydney." Shay met the older woman's eyes and saw nothing but forgiveness in their dark depths. "I don't deserve credit for this. I simply knocked down a few roadblocks so that you all could once again accomplish the amazing things that you do on a daily basis." It was difficult to gauge the group's thoughts on what she was saying, but their silence indicated that she had their undivided attention.

"I haven't taken the time in the past to tell you all how truly proud I am to work with such a gifted group of individuals, but I plan to change that going forward. As for today..." Shay took a cup of punch from the table and held it up to Sydney. "I want to tell you, Sydney, that you're a class act. You have no idea how much I appreciate all you've done. Good luck and I hope you're always treated like the lady that you are."

"Here, here!" Chase and Ray shouted in unison from the side of the room.

While her employees drank punch, ate cake and said their individual good-byes to Sydney, Shay exited the room to look for Angelo. She took a fresh cup of punch and a large piece of cake with her.

Angelo looked up from his desk as she entered his office. "Somebody's birthday?" he asked.

"Yours apparently." Shay set the treats down in front of him and took a seat.

"What're you up to now, Bennett?" He turned the cake around suspiciously. "Is this poisoned?"

"Tempting," Shay said, "but no."

"Then what's up?" Angelo succumbed to his famous sweet tooth and dug into the cake with relish.

"We solved the interface problem this morning. We've got a software program to deliver to Team Dynamics."

A huge Cheshire grin filled Angelo's round, red cheeks. "I knew you could do it, Bennett. You always perform great under pressure."

Shay wanted to punch him. "All the grief and threats you've been piling on me and this is all you have to say?" she pressed.

"Yeah." Angelo scooped up the remaining frosting on his plate with the side of the fork then licked the plastic utensil clean. "Course you scared me with that passing out thing last week. How're you feeling, by the way?"

"Fine, Angelo." Shay lifted herself from the chair. It was better if she left now; that way she could attempt to follow Jake's advice about not taking things so seriously. It would probably bring on an attack if she dwelled on Angelo's belated inquiry on her condition. "I'm doing just fine," she said to the king of insincerity.

"Good. I'll tell the powers that be that you didn't let us down after all." He picked up the phone as he swallowed the punch in one greedy gulp.

"You do that, Angelo. I think I'll take the rest of the day off." Shay closed the office door behind her so that she missed his reply. If he was going to insist that she stay, she wanted to have a valid reason for not obeying.

It took another good-bye to Sydney, a couple of phone calls and forty-five minutes before Shay actually was prepared to leave the office. It was just twelve-thirty and her stomach was loudly announcing its empty state.

Feeling a little adventurous, and a touch giddy, Shay decided to go to the deli before going home. She would surprise Jake by making lunch. It was safer than hopping into bed with him since she still hadn't reconciled her feelings for him. The elevator stopped, the doors opened, and Shay stood face-to-face with Cleo.

For a moment, Shay thought of making some excuse about forgetting something so she could turn tail and run. Instead, she entered the elevator and stood next to her ex-friend. It was better to deal with it, she decided. "Hi," she said, looking up at the numbers above the door, not expecting a reply.

"Hello," came Cleo's cool response.

The elevator stopped on the next two floors and Cleo moved to allow people and distance to come between them. Shay didn't blame her. By the time they reached the first floor, Shay had managed to find the courage to say more to Cleo. When they were both outside of the elevator, Shay caught her by the arm. "Hey, Cleo."

"What?" The short, stylish braids whipped around as Cleo turned to face Shay.

"Sunday is Jake's birthday." Shay found it hard to continue under Cleo's hard glare.

"And?"

Shay shrugged. "I thought it would be nice if you came over. Jake would like to see you."

"That's nice." Cleo's voice was pure ice. "And what about you? Do you want me to come over?"

Shay pleaded with her eyes and nodded her head. "I do."

Cleo sighed and looked around the busy lobby. "I don't

know—"

"Please," Shay took her leather-gloved hand. "I miss you, Cleo."

"I'll think about it." Water filled the woman's chocolate dark eyes before she headed quickly for the doors.

She'd tried. Pulling on her gloves, Shay buttoned her coat and exited the building. The sun was shining for the first time all week, though the air still carried the crisp bite of winter. It was such a beautiful day, Shay decided to walk the few blocks to the deli, then go home. The more she walked, the more she liked it and decided not to go home immediately.

She stopped at a boutique before she ever reached the deli, deciding that she needed a dress to wear to church on Sunday. It had been a long time since she'd gone to service. She was sure she had only business suits in her closet.

She found a lovely navy blue dress at that boutique and a pair of navy pumps to match at another. It was mid-afternoon by the time Shay decided her feet were too tired to enter another store.

Instead of a surprise lunch, she'd make pork chops for dinner. It seemed to be one of Jake's favorites and, since they were talking to each other again, she wanted to do everything in her power not to mess things up.

Jake was in the shower when she got home. "Dang it," Shay said aloud as she did a little jig by the door. She'd had to pee for the past two hours and her bladder felt as if it were about to explode. Quickly, she removed her coat and boots and went to knock on the bathroom door. "Jake?" she yelled so he could hear her. "I need to use the bathroom. Do you mind?"

"Shay?" he said on the other side of the door.

"Yeah. I need to use the bathroom," she repeated.

"There's a perfectly good cup on the table," he yelled and then began to laugh.

"Very funny." Shay entered the room, not caring if he minded or not. It was steamy inside, but she had no problem finding the toilet. She'd done it a thousand times in the middle of the night. "Don't look," she said, pulling down her panties and sighing with relief as her bladder emptied.

"Don't flush," Jake instructed from his side of the shower curtain. "I kind of like the way I look with unscalded skin."

She did too, but now wasn't the time to admit how badly she wanted to see the white lather against the baked brown of his chest. "Sorry, but I couldn't hold it any longer."

Jake peeked from around the curtain. "I know just how

you feel."

Any other time, Shay would have been mortified to be seen with her underwear dropped to her ankles and her skirt hitched up to her waist, but Jake had seen her naked and had admired her lovingly from every angle. Even now, his gaze lingered much longer than necessary.

When he retreated behind the curtain once more, Shay quickly finished her business and adjusted her clothes. As she washed her hands, Jake turned off the shower and stepped out of the tub. As usual, he was comfortable with his nakedness and didn't seem the least disconcerted with the fact that she was staring at him as if he were the last piece of chocolate in the box.

He grabbed the towel from the rack and rubbed it across his chest. "Would you mind drying my back?" he asked, offering the terry cloth to her.

Accepting the towel, Shay shook her head. Using both hands, she first dried the width of his broad shoulders then drew the towel down his back until her hands met at the swell of his well-shaped behind. Since the opportunity had presented itself, she took the liberty of drying both of his cheeks as well. "How's that," she asked, hoping he'd ask her to continue.

"Great." He turned around to retrieve the now damp towel. "Thanks." He held her eyes with his lusty gaze for a moment and then slowly dried his legs and finally his pelvic area in slow circles. "Excuse me," he said, opening the door behind her. "I've got to get dressed."

He was teasing her and Shay was tempted to follow him to his room. She was more than certain that, this time, she'd be screaming the right name. Today, all she could think of was Jake. But she had some unfinished business to tend to on Sunday. Maybe next week she could completely untangle her feelings and literally and figuratively be in bed with only one man.

Shay left the bathroom, gave a longing look at Jake's semi-open door and went to the kitchen. The pork chops were waiting.

Chapter Fourteen

Jake struggled with his tie for the fourth time that morning. The knot still didn't look right. If he did see his mama today, he wanted her to find him presentable. It was hard to believe he hadn't seen her in ten years. The only news he'd had of her was what Jerome had told him during his visits and what her friend Pruda Daniels had told him at the subway stop.

She hadn't opened her door to him when he'd first gotten out of prison, but maybe, if she saw him today, she would speak to him. That's all he wanted; just to speak to her.

Finishing with his tie, he stepped back from the dresser mirror in his room and studied his reflection.

He looked good in his brother's navy tailored suit and blue dress shirt. He imagined Jerome wearing it and could almost feel his presence. It was comforting.

Jake frowned into the mirror. "It's just this tie, Rome. What's up with it?" The navy material looked lopsided, as if a child had attempted the knot. "Shay!" Maybe she could help him figure out what he was doing wrong. "What do you know about ties?"

Her no-nonsense heels came down the hallway to his room. "What did you say?" she asked entering his room.

Jake looked at her and his mouth dropped to the floor. She wore a navy blue dress with a scalloped neckline that revealed the lush lines of her cleavage. The sleeves were sheer to the wrist and her narrow waist and full hips filled the remainder of the dress in erotic ways. "Shay-Shay, Bay-Bay," he chanted. "You sure make that dress look good."

Shay smiled and lifted some of his doubts that today would be a good day. "You don't look half bad yourself," she said. "Now, what were you hollerin' about?" She crossed her arms and shifted her weight to one shapely leg.

It took Jake a minute to remember. "Oh. Can you help me with this tie? It looks all wrong."

Shay came over and loosened the cloth around his neck. She smelled absolutely wonderful. It was a perfume scent he hadn't smelled on her before. Unfortunately, Jake now had a magnificent view of her cleavage and was mesmerized once more by the trail of small tattooed tears that slid between her soft mounds. He was tempted for a moment to forget about church.

"You just haven't done this in a while. Lost your touch," Shay said. She bit the corner of her lip as she manipulated the tie. "Keep your chin up," she ordered.

Jake obeyed. It was best he didn't commit any sins right before going to church...even if he could ask for forgiveness.

"There you go." Shay patted the tie and turned him to face the mirror. "Better?"

Jake grinned at the perfect knot. "Much. Thanks."

Shay stepped back and looked at him for a moment. "Nervous?"

Jake filled his cheeks with air and blew it out hard. "Yeah," he admitted.

"Why? Because you haven't seen her in so long?"

"Partially. But what if..." Jake was a little embarrassed to tell her the rest.

"What if she still doesn't want to see you?" Shay finished.

Jake nodded and placed his hands in his pockets.

"Then you do what you do to me and everybody else." Shay walked over and placed a hand on his cheek. "Forgive her."

Jake held her hand to his cheek for a moment longer, then kissed her palm before letting her go.

"Let me grab my purse and I'll be ready."

As Shay's footsteps made their way down the hall, Jake remembered that he had one more item to collect himself. He slid open the top drawer of his dresser and plucked the small package sitting in the midst of his sock rolls. Carefully he placed it inside his jacket pocket before meeting Shay in the living room.

The sight of Shay's curves in that blue dress was no less provoking the second time around. Not that Jake cared about such things, but the woman was sure going to look fine next to him going up the church aisle.

Jake pulled Shay's coat from the rack and held it open for her.

"I can put my own coat—"

"Would you let a man help you with your coat, please?" Jake remained unmoved.

"All right," Shay acquiesced. "You wanna help me with my gloves and hat, too?" she asked facetiously.

With a dramatic sigh, Jake took the gloves and pushed them onto her long fingers one at a time. Then he placed her hat on her head, careful of the barrettes she'd placed on either side to keep her wild ringlets off her face.

Shay grinned under his attention.

Someone knocked on the door just as Jake pulled on his

own coat. "Expecting company?" he asked.

Cleo was outside, bundled up in her faux fur coat.

"Cleo." Jake threw his arms around her. "It's good to see you."

When the hug ended, Cleo's eyes fell to Shay. Her bright smile dimmed. "Jake said you were going to church today. Do you mind?"

"Not at all," Shay said. In fact, she was thrilled that Cleo had showed up, even if it was just for Jake.

The cab ride to the church was uncomfortable. Shay sat next to Cleo who sat next to Jake. It was foolish, but Shay was a little jealous as the two of them chatted about the comic books they'd read as kids. They both couldn't wait to see Spiderman. It was also clear Jake had called Cleo to invite her to church well before Shay had invited her to celebrate his birthday. Had he been hedging his bets by inviting them both, thinking that one of them would turn him down?

Get real, Shay. She looked at him and how happy he seemed to be, not at all concerned that he had both of them in the cab. He'd done this on purpose. He'd counted on both of them saying yes to him so that they had an opportunity to make up with one another.

Shay frowned and turned her attention outside the cab window. She hated being manipulated. How dare Jake try to manage her friendship with Cleo? She was perfectly able to handle her own business. Much later, they would have to have words about this.

The cab driver traversed the tired streets of the inner city and pulled up in front of Trinity Baptist. It stood as proud as ever with its red brick exterior, A-shaped roof and white cross acting as a homing device for its flock.

The inside had changed slightly, Jake noticed. The carpet was new and the old wooden pews now had cushions. But along both sides of the church there were still the amazing stained glass windows turning shards of sunlight into colored streams that fell upon the sanctuary.

An older woman with wide hips and a pleasantly round dark face held out a white-gloved hand, beckoning Jake to follow her. Several members of the congregation stole curious glances as they moved down the aisle. It must've been because they were new faces... or perhaps because of the two beautiful women he escorted. Jake had to admit that they were both knockouts this morning.

As they settled into a pew, Jake looked around. He didn't recognize any of the faces, though he thought he should.

Not even Pruda Daniels could be found and the church was nearly full.

The choir came in from behind the altar and filled the half circle of seats behind the pastor's chair. To Jake's surprise, they had a whole band accompanying them now and the songs of praise were no longer solemn, but joyful. The last time he had been here, they had only a piano and organ and sang only from the hymnal. The choir director instructed them to rise to their feet and had the place rocking and praising Jesus in no time flat.

Jake glanced back at the door several times. By the time the pastor took the pulpit, he had resigned himself to the fact that today wasn't the day he would see his mother. He let his disappointment fade as he joined the others in an opening prayer.

In the middle of the prayer, Shay nudged him. "Jake," she whispered.

Jake frowned and looked at her from the corner of his nearly closed eyes. "What?"

"Look who's here," she said with a wide smile. "Let me by."

As Shay maneuvered her way to the right side of him next to Cleo, Jake looked to his left. His mother was excusing herself as she made her way down the aisle to him with Miss

Pruda Daniels nearly pushing her from behind.

Jake was overwhelmed. By the time she reached his side, his arms were ready to wrap her up and hold her close. "Mama. I'm so glad to see you." She smelled just the way he remembered, like Jean Naté bath splash. Her black wavy hair was in two braids tucked under her Sunday hat like always, but now there were strands of gray woven into the thick plaits. She seemed thinner, but maybe it was because he'd grown bigger over the years.

"I'm sorry, baby. I'm so sorry," she wept into his chest.

Jake shushed her. "You have nothing to apologize for. Just let me hold you a while, Mama. That's all I want. That's all I want."

Because she wept in his arms, Jake wept also. He didn't know how much he'd missed his mother's love until that very moment. He didn't ever want to lose it again.

After a while, he felt Shay patting his back gently. Jake opened his eyes to see the rest of the congregation sitting with all eyes resting on him and his mother. Some were wiping tears from their eyes; others were nodding and sending blessings their way.

Jake released his mother from the hug. He helped her out of her coat and into the seat beside him so that the pastor could proceed with his sermon. He took her hand, not ready to lose contact.

Shay reached across him and handed his mother a tissue to wipe her eyes and nose. Jake then took the one she offered to him and did the same.

Jake only half listened to the sermon. He was far too distracted by the loving looks he shared with his mother, her constant patting of his hand, his arm, his cheek. Every glance, every touch, every tear she caught with her tissue told him that she loved him. That she'd always loved him. It was the best gift Jake could've received on his birthday.

Our birthday, he reminded himself. But it didn't feel the same without Jerome. Jake didn't plan to celebrate the day. Instead he wanted to take the opportunity to finally say good-bye to his brother. Maybe then, he'd stop the strange sensations he was experiencing more and more frequently.

It took a while to leave the church after services ended. It seemed that everyone stopped to say something to Olivia Masters and her son. Olivia had never been more proud. She'd stood before her son in shame this morning. He'd gone to prison and she'd forsaken him in his time of need. Turned her back on her own blood and left him without her love all because her pride had taken a blow ten years ago.

But her son had looked upon her with love and forgiveness today. He'd wrapped her in his strong arms and told her that he loved her. She didn't deserve him, but she was so very proud of him and thankful for him.

Jake was saying his thanks to Pruda. The old biddy had given Olivia a million miles of grief this morning before she'd finally agreed to come to church. Olivia had dragged her heels, making them late, anything to stop the freight train of Pruda's determination. She'd lost. She'd thank her old friend later over coffee.

Jake helped all of them into their coats, then huddled them inside the foyer. Olivia could tell by the way his eyebrows came together and his mouth turned down that what he was about to say was serious. His skinny frame had filled out and his face had taken on a mature handsomeness over the years, but his expression was the same as always.

"I've asked Shay already, but I was wondering if all of you would do me the favor of visiting Ground Zero with me today. I never got a chance to say good-bye to Jerome and since that's where he died..." Jake stopped to clear his throat. "Anyway...it would mean a lot to me."

Olivia dropped her head and closed her eyes. Why did he have to go and ask that? It'd been hard enough facing up to one son, now it looked like she'd have to have a reckoning with the other. Olivia took a deep breath, knowing she needed to do this. "I'll go with you, son," she said, taking his hand.

"Thank you, Mama." Jake kissed her cheek.

"I already told you, I'd go," Shay said softly.

Jake nodded and turned his attention to the darker woman. "What do you say, Cleo?"

Olivia had never met her before, but she thought it must mean a lot to Jake that she go, considering the way he was squeezing her hand while he waited for an answer.

Finally, the woman stopped looking everywhere but straight and said she would go. Before anybody had the chance to change their minds, Jake had them outside and ushered into two separate cabs.

To her joy, Olivia shared a cab with Jake while Shay and the Cleo woman shared the other. She wanted some one-on-one time with her son to confess all her sins to him so he would know what he was forgiving. He was making this way too easy on her when she knew she deserved to suffer at least a little bit.

Shay didn't know if she was more nervous about visiting the site where Jerome had died or about being alone in a cab with Cleo. Shay focused her attention on the passing landscape outside the window. The snow hadn't completely melted from the last storm, but foot traffic, cars and time had transformed God's pristine blanket of white into dreary, ugly brown sludge.

After a few miles had passed, Shay realized that the words she needed to say wouldn't be found out there. She looked over at her friend, who seemed to be searching for the same answers on her side of the cab. Shay cleared her throat to get her attention. "Hey, Cleo?"

Cleo turned. Her face was full of confusion and concern. Her eyes held questions, but she didn't say a word.

"I want to say that I'm sorry." Shay couldn't meet Cleo's eyes so she pulled nervously at her gloves instead. "I said some pretty mean things to you and—"

"You're sorry." Cleo finished Shay's thought matter-of-factly and then turned away.

Shay's heartbeat quickened as she realized that Cleo was too hurt to make this easy. She'd have to try harder. "I know I don't deserve your forgiveness—"

"You sure don't." Cleo's voice broke and she took a few deep breaths. "All you care about is yourself, Shay. You never cared about me or Jerome."

Her contempt hurt Shay deeply. "I am selfish," she admitted tearfully. "But I did care about Jerome and I do care about you, Cleo."

Cleo turned on her. "How can you say that? Now that I look back at it, you were manipulating me, weren't you? You told me how madly in love with Jerome you were to keep me away. Isn't that right?"

Shay nodded and fumbled in her purse for Kleenex. "I wanted so bad for him to love me, Cleo. I'd wanted him to love me since we were kids. It just hurt that he didn't want me, that he preferred almost anybody but me. It got so much worse, when he stopped dating everyone and started to sneak around to see you."

"Why?"

"Because he loved you and I was jealous. I was afraid I would have no one again. That I would be alone."

"So you made sure that none of us were happy?" Cleo nearly spat the question. "To think how guilty Jerome and I felt..." She shook her head and burst into tears.

Shay caught a glimpse of the cab driver's curious glance in

the rearview mirror. She didn't care. Let the whole world see what a mess she'd made of things; it couldn't hurt any worse. "I would do anything to make it right, Cleo, but I can't. It's too late and..." Shay couldn't finish because she was crying too hard.

Each of them retreated to nurse the wounds that were now fully open. As they finally reached their location, Shay tried to bring herself under control without much success.

Jake opened the door to help her out and concern draped his features as he looked from one of them to the other. "What happened?"

Shay just shook her head and exited the cab. She didn't want to talk about it.

A few curious tourists were at the site, taking pictures and talking off-handedly about the attack of September 11th. The fact that they could talk so unemotionally about it was testament to the fact that they had not lost any loved ones to the disaster. But as Shay fell behind Jake and his mother and advanced closer to the place where the Twin Towers had stood, she felt a strangeness overtake her.

Silence seized their small party as they each looked over the area. Shay knew that this would be a day she would never be able to forget.

Chapter Fifteen

Ground Zero remained a restricted area. Much of the wreckage had been cleared but there was a great emptiness now where the structures had previously filled the sky.

Jake approached as far as the police tape and hazard cones would permit. He thought of his brother being here, saving lives...and losing his own. Jerome had died a hero and Jake knew that his brother wouldn't have had it any other way. "Jerome always told me that he would rather die doing something big rather than go quietly in his sleep," he said aloud to the others.

"He dreamed of being a fireman all his life, but could never score high enough on the exams. Every time he visited me he had a new story to tell about how he would improve and make it in the next year." Jake looked skyward into the clouds. "You passed the test on September 11th, bro. You saved lives. You made a difference. No one can score higher than that."

His mother cried softly at his side. "It was my fault he died," she choked on her sobs.

"Don't be silly, Mama." Jake put an arm around her shoulders.

"It is," she insisted. "I was too proud to stand by you, Jacob. I abandoned you, turned my back on you when you needed me and showed God that I didn't deserve my sons. When Jerome died, I thought I was being punished. I thought I had lost both of you forever."

With her words shattering his heart, Jake tried to comfort her. His tears streamed down his face as he bid his brother a silent good-bye and tried to convince her mother that this wasn't her doing.

"It's me who should be guilty, Mama Olivia," Shay sobbed. "I took the one thing from him that he wanted more than anything else. He'd found the woman he loved and I made him feel guilty for wanting to be with her." She nearly doubled over with grief.

Jake worried that she would suffer another anxiety attack and moved around his mother to stand next to her. Before he reached her side, Cleo was there, hugging her tightly.

He stopped short, deciding to give them the moment. Hopefully they would begin healing their friendship. When the embrace ended, Jake decided it was time to pull out his package.

"I found something in Jerome's room," he announced soberly. "I brought it with me, because I think it's only fitting to close out this chapter on his life and start us all moving forward." He handed the package to Cleo.

Brushing the remaining tears from her face quickly, she accepted the tiny box and card from Jake with trembling hands. She fumbled awkwardly with the card, until Shay reached out a hand to her.

"Let me get that for you, sweetie," Shay offered.

Cleo handed it over and turned the box around in her palm as if she didn't know what to do with it.

"It's just a note to himself," Shay said, looking at the small 3x5 card. It's dated September 1, 2001. He's written Cleopatra Masters, my future wife."

Cleo wiped more tears from her face. She handed the box to Shay. "I can't..."

Struggling to keep her own emotions in check, Shay opened the box for her friend and turned it so she could see the ring inside. "It's gorgeous, Cleo."

Jake stepped in then. He removed the ring from the box and held out his hand for Cleo's. She pulled off her leather glove and placed her palm in his.

He slid the ring on her finger and held her hand for a long moment. "Would you be my honorary sister-in-law?"

Cleo admired the pear shaped diamond that grandly reflected the meager offering of sunlight and smiled. "I will."

As silence fell among the group once again, it seemed that there was no more to say. Jake looked back at the wreckage and reached a hand out to the air as if he could feel his brother's touch in return. He felt nothing but the breeze blow across his palm. "Gotta go, bro," he said and once again took his mother's hand.

"I've got greens and a roast cooking for dinner," Olivia offered. "If you want to come over."

Jake smiled. "I love pot roast."

Olivia looked back at Shay and Cleo who were now walking arm-in-arm. "You girls can come along, too."

They agreed.

Jake was satisfied. The day had worked out better than he'd hoped.

❁

His mother's cooking was better than Jake remembered.

The tensions between Cleo and Shay evaporated over the sweet potato pie. By the time he and Shay returned home, Jake was spent by the emotions of the day. After shedding his coat and hat, he collapsed on the couch.

"I don't even have the energy to click the remote," he confessed.

"Pretty tiring day, huh?" Shay disappeared inside her bedroom.

Jake laid his head back on the couch and closed his eyes. His body felt heavy, as if he'd been drugged or beaten to the point of exhaustion. Just before sleep took hold, Shay was standing in front of him, changed into her robe.

Jake wasn't too tired to wonder if she had anything on beneath. "What's up?" he asked, sensing she had something she wanted to say.

"We have some unfinished business." She was holding his bottle of Super Six oil.

Intrigued, Jake forced himself to sit up. "If it involves a massage, I'll kiss your feet."

She smiled. "Assume the position."

Together they moved the coffee table and threw the couch cushions on the floor. Jake disrobed down to his BVDs in record time. "Should we put some towels down?" he asked.

"Don't wanna get oil on the cushions."

"Use this." Shay removed her robe and threw it down.

Jake forgot to be tired when he saw the black lace underwear. "Have you been wearing that all day?"

"Lie down," she ordered.

She didn't have to ask twice. When her oiled fingers
touched his tired back, Jake moaned. Her palms moving in
slow, deliberate circles from his shoulders to the small of his
back was like a slice of heaven. In contrast, her soft thighs
straddling his bottom he found sexy as hell. The impact of
such extremes colliding all in one place created a reaction he
couldn't stop. Jake smiled, wondering why he would ever
want to.

To his surprise, Shay was patient and thorough as she
moved her magical hands over every inch of his backside. By
the time she finished with his legs, Jake was thoroughly
relaxed and completely horny.

"Okay." She eased off him so that he could move. "Turn
over."

"You don't want me to do that," Jake warned.

"Why? Do you think I'd be surprised?" she teased.

"Okay. You asked for it." Jake shifted on the cushions and
rolled onto his back. Placing his hands behind his head, he

watched her reaction.

Her eyes roamed his chest and fell to his groin. His BVDs could no longer contain his entire length, but Shay didn't say a word. Instead, she poured more oil onto her hand and heated it between her palms.

"I see you're not surprised," Jake observed.

"I was surprised the first time." She placed her hands on his chest and began a slow, sensuous massage. Her hands moved and pushed down the material to reveal the rest of him. "This time I'm merely saying thanks."

Jake felt a fog roll through his brain as her hot slick fingers slid up and down his sensitive flesh. "I hope you know what you're starting, woman."

"You challenged me earlier this week. I'm giving you my answer."

Jake opened one eye. "Talking about the kiss?"

"Uh, huh."

He closed his eye once more and smiled. "That was some of my best work," he bragged.

"I'll say." Her fingers never stopped.

Jake was nearing the point of no return. "So, you're ready for this?"

"I think so."

Jake grabbed her hands and pulled her slowly down on top of him. When they were eye-to-eye and pelvis-to-pelvis, he told her, "I need you to be sure."

Her eyes softened but never blinked. "I am sure, Jake. There's only one man for me. Always has been, I just didn't know it until now."

At that moment, the day became a complete success. Jake thought that maybe now was the time to celebrate his birthday. "There's one thing I've always known, too." He kissed her gently, loving the way she tasted.

"What's that?"

"That you would look great in black lace."

Shay's smile warmed every corner of his heart. "I'd be embarrassed to know how long you've been thinking that, wouldn't I?" she asked.

"Oh, yeah." Jake pushed his fingers into the thick of her curls and brought her mouth over his. She tasted even better than he remembered and Jake tried his best to devour the sweet candy of her mouth.

She pulled away before he was ready. Jake started to protest, but stopped when he saw her reach for the front clasp on her bra.

"You may like this stuff, but it's a little scratchy. Do you mind?"

"Go ahead," he encouraged, pulling his hands from behind his head in preparation for the treat of her soft flesh.

Her breasts sprang free from the flimsy cloth and Jake immediately filled his awaiting hands. He rolled her chocolate kiss nipples between his fingers and delighted as they hardened.

Shay pulled away once again and stood over him. "These are a little uncomfortable, too," she explained. Her voice was soft and sexy as she pushed the delicate fabric down her fabulous legs.

"You're staring," she teased.

"I'm dreaming," he corrected, running his hands up and down her legs. "If you wake me up, I'll kill ya."

"You won't kill me." She lowered herself in slow, undulating motions down to his crotch. "Because you're not a violent man, Jake Masters. You're kind." She kissed him. "You're forgiving." She kissed him again. "And I love you."

It was her turn to deliver the kiss that killed and soon Jake wasn't capable of rational thought. He ran his hands along her back and bottom while he enjoyed the weight of her softly scented body.

Jake couldn't get enough of her and rolled until she was

beneath him. He assaulted her breasts with kisses and suck-led the erect tips of her nipples like a kid with a lollipop. There was no explaining why he enjoyed them so damned much and he didn't dwell too long in trying to figure it out.

While paying homage to her breasts, Jake found the tears once more. In the dim lamplight, he traced a finger from the top of her breasts and followed the trail inside. "Five lone-ly little teardrops," he said aloud. He adjusted himself so that he could look at Shay's eyes. "What do they mean?"

"I'll tell you later." Shay reached up to kiss him.

Jake pulled back. "No more secrets. Tell me why they're there." He continued to trace his finger along the little trail.

Shay looked toward the ceiling, seeming to recall the rea-son. " You know what my childhood was like. My mother was drunk all the time and had strange people over to the house."

Jake nodded. "I remember. You missed a lot of school."

"I spent a lot of time hiding from my mother and crying, feeling sorry for myself."

If it hadn't been for your mother…" She shook her head. "Anyway, one day I decided I was done with feeling sorry for myself, done with tears. I needed to be strong. I had the tears tattooed there as a a reminder never to cry again. And I always remembered, Jake," she said in a tortured voice. "Until Jerome died… and that day you found me here on the floor."

"It's okay to cry, Shay." Jake moved up and kissed just her lips. "There's no shame in it." He caught the tears at the corners of her eyes with this thumbs and wiped them away. "Sometimes their purpose is to cleanse our souls."

"If that's the case, I've got the cleanest soul on earth today." Shay managed a sad grin.

"Let's put the sad stuff away, all right? There's still a few hours left to my birthday and I wanna have some fun."

"Then shut up and let me love you, Jake." She wrapped her arms around his neck and her legs around his hips and she kissed him as if tomorrow would never come.

Jake rose from the floor with her limbs wrapped tightly around him and carried her to her bed. Wasting no time, he found his way inside her sweet walls, squeezing his eyes tight because of how good she felt. This time their lovemaking wasn't sweet and sensuous but urgent and raw. Their pace was fast, punctuated with grunts, groans and moans. Jake went insane each time Shay's hips pushed against him. His body was on edge, reveling in the feeling of lust gone mad.

Powerful, that's how he felt. Powerful, strong and fierce.

Yet he knew that at any moment, Shay could bring him to his knees. It might be the squeeze of her wet walls or the calling of his name or the movement of her hips that would push him over the edge. He wanted it. But not yet. He wasn't ready yet to end this feeling. Not ready yet to relinquish this power. Not ready.

Shay had never felt more alive than she did at this moment. The walls of shame, of embarrassment, all the walls she'd ever built around her heart were completely destroyed. Jake had brought them down with his kindness and forgiveness and persistence…and one everlasting gobstopper of a kiss.

Forcing him to change positions, Shay was now on top and in control. Jake's hands gripped her hips, encouraging her movements while his mouth moved hungrily from one breast to the other. Shay loved the way he made her feel. Loved that he made no apologies for desiring every inch of her. When he moaned, she repeated the motion. If he cried out, she moved even faster. She wanted this birthday to be the one he would always remember. She did her best to tattoo the moment forever in his mind and his body.

Jake cursed and tensed as he squeezed her bottom in desperation. Shay could feel him pumping inside of her and kept moving until she found her own nirvana. She screamed his name at the top of her lungs. Screamed it twice so that every neighbor could hear. She loved Jacob Masters and they all had a right to know.

Collapsing on top of him, Shay couldn't tell whose heart beat the fastest or who panted the hardest. All she knew was that she'd never felt so free. "So what do you say?" she asked after she'd caught enough breath to speak. "Did I hold up my end of the bargain?"

Jake gave her a playful pat on the bottom. "I'd say it was a good beginning," he teased.

"Beginning?" Shay sat up and swatted his chest. "Everyone in the apartment building could hear me screaming your name. Besides, I nearly killed you, man."

"I'll have to admit, I am a little winded." Jake's broad grin put his dimples on display. "And you tattooed the hell out of my—"

Shay covered his mouth with her hand long enough to replace it with her lips. "It's Sunday. You shouldn't curse on Sunday."

"In that case," his voice softened, "let me give thanks for all my blessings." His kisses were gentle as he rolled her to his side. When his kisses ended, Shay rested her head on his shoulder and listened as his breathing deepened into slumber.

For the first time since forever, Shay closed her eyes in the dark and no nasty memories of her mother surfaced. No worries about work played through her mind. No desire for liquor to soothe her guilt and loneliness, the tiger that was her anxiety had retracted his claws and Shay hoped it would never return.

Tomorrow and all her future tomorrows would be better now that she had Jake by her side. She had faith in the person she'd become because of him and knew that she would never let herself down again.

Choose from

The BEST Of The BEST

Upcoming
Genesis Titles

Excerpts of
Tommorow's Promise
an upcoming release
by
Leslie Esdaile

The sound of the children getting up and the movements of the house hadn't awakened her. She'd been up for hours, already showered, packed for Beijing, and was looking off the balcony by the time she heard Wendell and Carol's keys in the apartment door.

Fatigue was battling within the internal provinces of her mind, body, and spirit. Her body still hurt from denying it instant gratification; her heart felt heavy because she missed him-no matter that they'd just met, or her brain kept giving her facts that she was well-versed in. But she still couldn't come to a peace accord that was acceptable to her body and heart. She wanted to make love to this man in the worst way, but felt like it was way too soon to do that.

Sleep had been fitful at best and had run away with first light, anticipation over seeing him again chasing it from her, and now she needed to talk to her brother.

Somehow she had to give Mark clearance to join them without offending her brother, who had given her the visit to China in the first place. Time was all out of sync. Mark had been right; if this were only months later. Complex didn't even begin to describe it.

"Good morning," Carol said in a slow, cheerful voice, yawning as she knocked and entered the bedroom without waiting for Tina to respond.

Tina smiled and came in off the balcony. "How was your date?"

Carol sighed and sat down on the bed. "Marvelous, and the flowers were gorgeous. Thank you."

"I'm the one who should be thanking you... the dress was beautiful, and all the stuff that went with it. Thank you, Sis."

Carol covered her mouth and chuckled. "Oh, yeah, I almost forgot. I'm so glad you liked it."

Tina found herself chuckling with Carol as she crossed the room and leaned against the wall. "It looks like you got hit with a dose of your own medicine."

"Oh, yeah..." Carol breathed. "I didn't realize how long it had been since it was just the two of us."

"Must be nice," Tina whispered. "You both deserve it."

Carol patted the side of the bed for Tina to join her. When she did, Carol leaned her head on Tina's shoulder and let out a sigh of contentment that said it all.

"I know I seem silly, but I'm still crazy about your brother after all these years."

"That doesn't seem so crazy. You guys are still practically newly weds."

Carol eased her body to lie on her side on the bed and placed her hand under her head as she leaned on her elbow. Tina turned and sat sidesaddle, watching Carol trace her finger in the pattern of the comforter.

"How was last night?"

Carol hadn't looked up as she asked the question, and by the way she was tracing a lazy pattern, Tina could tell that it was a loaded one. To her surprise, her own finger began tracing a slow, repetitive pattern of its own.

"I'm crazy about him."

"Good."

Neither woman looked up.

"It was a near miss, last night."

"Good," Carol whispered, smiling but still not looking up."

"It's too soon, though. You know what I mean?"

"Maybe, maybe not."

"That's the dilemma."

"He's going to Beijing with us, isn't he?"

"How'd you know?" Tina stared at the top of Carol's hair, but still Carol didn't look up.

"I knew he would."

"How do you know these things?"

"It was all over his face when he told us he'd take you for the rest of the afternoon."

"Oh."

"I worked on Wendell. Softened him up real good." Carol giggled.

Tina chuckled. "You are treacherous, Sis."

"I know," Carol replied, grinning. "You didn't sleep well last night, did you?"

Tina glanced away. "Not really."

"Neither did we," Carol chuckled and pushed herself up. "I'm finished then."

"Why?" Tina said, suddenly panicked. The odd sensation hit her out of the blue. She wasn't prepared for Carol's withdrawal from the situation so soon-even though she'd struggled with her meddling. Now she would be left to her own devices, just dangling by a thread.

"Because you don't need my help any more. We'd be third wheels."

"But how do I know if this isn't just chemical?"

"You don't."

"That's the thing."

"You never do. Did you interview him?"

"Yes," Tina murmured.

"Did you like the answers he gave to your questions?"

"Yes."

"Did he interview you?"

"Yes."

"Did he seem to like the answers to your questions?"

Tina glanced toward the balcony. "I think so."

"You have a background check-and he checks out from this side. You do from his side. Why are you so afraid, then?"

"I don't know." Truthfully the word afraid, now exposed to the air, said out loud, resonated inside of her. Carol defined a part of the pang. She'd put language to the emotion.

"Tina, you don't like to fail. It isn't even in your vocabulary, is it."

She shook her head no and kept her gaze cast out the window.

"And this guy, unlike the others, feels like he's a risk-not because he did anything wrong, but because he's doing everything right... and it's scaring the crap out of you, because if you drop your guard and you totally give in, and he pulls back, you're scared you won't be able to pull back for the first time in your life. Right?"

Tina's arms found themselves wrapped around her own body and she bit her bottom lip.

"Wow," Carol sighed. "You've got it bad, kiddo."

When the phone rang, they both stared at each other.

"I place a week's salary on a wager that it's him."

"No, probably not. He said he might go along with the three of us to-"

"He's going. Trust me."

Wendell paced into the bedroom, holding the cordless phone. "Hey, Sis. Good morning. It's for you."

"You owe me," Carol chuckled, standing slowly, stretching with a yawn. "Tell Mark we said 'Hi.'"

She waited until the bedroom door closed and then brought the telephone to her ear. A hundred thoughts raced through her brain at once. Part of her was trying to keep her heart from beating with an erratic pulse. What if he'd changed his mind? Then again, what if he hadn't?

"Hello."

"Hi."

"Hi."

"Have you eaten yet?"

"No. You?"

"No."

"Maybe we can grab something after everybody gets together?"

"Yeah. That would be nice."

"What time is your flight?"

"This afternoon at four."

"Do you have your information handy? Maybe I can get on the same one–if you still want me to go?"

"Yeah," she murmured, getting up to look for her folder on the dresser and then giving him the requested information.

"Okay," he murmured. "I guess I should come over and ask Wendell if he doesn't mind if I tag along?"

"Okay," she said softly.

"I can get a room in the same place where you guys will be... I mean, that way, we can all save time on convening when we go places."

"Yeah... that could work, let me give you the hotel." She stood and again went to consult the information on her dresser and gave it to him in very detached terms while she tried to keep her stomach from doing the weird little flip-flops it was doing.

"I had a really wonderful time with you last night," he said so quietly that she almost had to strain to hear his voice. "But I won't, uh, I mean to say that... I won't pressure you. Seriously. I was outta line, and things got outta hand... and I'm sorry if I came on a little strong. If you'd rather that I not go, or like, maybe, we could go out once you come back home stateside, well, uh, I'd under-stand."

Then there was the damnable silence. It hung between them

like a yellow caution light. Speak now or forever hold your peace, it flashed.

"No. I'd like you to come with us. Uh, it took two to, uh, well… it was on both sides-so no apology needed. I owe you one, and uh, if you feel uncomfortable now, and would rather wait until we were in our own space to go out, to uh, try to see if, well, maybe we could go out then, that is okay, too. But if you want to come with us, I have no problem with that."

Silence. Why hadn't she just said, 'Look, I'm crazy about you, and was about a hare's breath from going back to The Peace Hotel with you.' Stupid! She yelled at herself as the silence wound a new layer of tension through her and made it hard to breathe.

What was on his mind? Why didn't he just tell the woman that he was crazy about her, couldn't sleep all night because of her, and that he'd take any part of her company that she'd offer at the moment? All he had to do was say it!

"Put Wendell on the telephone, please. I'll see you in about an hour, and we can all eat, do he Old French Concession area and hit a few monuments before the flight. Okay?"

"Yeah, okay. See you in a few, 'bye."

"Yeah, see you in a few. 'Bye."

She stood slowly and walked through the apartment to find Wendell in the kitchen drinking a cup of coffee. She extended the telephone to him and he accepted it from her with a quizzical look.

"He wants to talk to you."

He paced in the apartment lobby waiting for Wendell to come downstairs. This was madness. The expression on his best friend's face said it all. Wendell had this concerned, what-the-hell-is-going-on-that-we-have-to-talk-outside kind of look when the elevator doors opened. In truth, he didn't know what he was going to say to the man. He'd prepared all sorts of openings to the discussion, but the expression on Wendell's face rendered all of them moot.

"You okay?"

"Uh. Yeah. Uh. Can we go get a cup of coffee?"

"We have coffee upstairs, man. You look like they just called you for special ops,. What's up? Why didn't you come upstairs?"

"Let's walk. Cool?"

"All right."

The two block walk in silence was both a blessing and a curse, and as they slipped into the local Starbucks café, neither of them went to the register to order, but found a table, immediately sat down, and looked at each other.

"This may be hard for you to believe, but I'm going to ask you to hear me out." Mark's statement had come out so fast, on such a straight path to Wendell's senses, that his friend sat back in his chair and rubbed his chin.

"Wow. Carol said this mess was serious."

"It is. Look, I wasn't prepared for it. Okay. And, and... and-"

"You're freaking."

"Yeah. In a word."

"Why?"

"She's your sister."

"Right."

"Right." He stared at Wendell hard. "I respect you, man. You know that. Right?"

"You'd better." Wendell offered a tense chuckle. "So, what happened that you've extracted me from my home to sit across the table to tell me what?"

"Nothing."

"Then what are we talking about?"

"Can I go to Beijing with you?"

"I cannot stop a grown man from air travel to-"

"That's not what I mean, and you know it."

Wendell studied the pattern in the wood table. "Don't play with her, okay."

"I'm not."

"Then why are you freaking and trying to get my blessing?"

Mark let his breath out hard and cast his focus out the window.

"I never felt like this about... It's too soon. You know?"

Wendell looked up and the motion drew Mark's line of vision to connect with his friend's stare.

"Are you telling me that you're hit?"

"I think so, man. But I can't tell."

"How deep is the wound?"

"I can't feel my legs. I'm not coherent."

They both laughed.

"Whatchu gonna do about it?"

"That's just the thing, I don't know?"

"You asking me to talk to her?"

"Vouch for me, man-so she doesn't think I'm playing games."

Wendell stared at him and smiled.

"You need some air. Paramedics are on the way."

"I'm serious, dude."

"I know, 'cause in all these years, I've never seen you like this. You brought her back respectfully last night, didn't you?"

"Of course, man!" Mark shot up from his chair and was now pacing.

"Sit down." Wendell chuckled. "Oh, I definitely believe you now."

"Look... she wants me to come to Beijing with you guys... I want to come to Beijing... hell, I don't know who brought it up first-but I know you haven't seen her in years, and this is for all intents and purposes, your family visit. I was just supposed to be here for a few days, to see the plant, maybe take your visiting family member around a little bit when you and Carol got tied up with the kids. But this has morphed into something that, I, for the life of me, had no intentions on... I was blindsided, man. This didn't go down like it was supposed to. And it's all truncated in this short time factor... and, I just want to be sure that you and I are on the same page, and are still cool."

He found himself breathing hard as he stood over the table while Wendell sat, and he glanced around at a few patrons who'd raised an eyebrow when his voice escalated.

"Sit," Wendell commanded in a quiet, pleasant tone. "Chill."

When he complied, Wendell leaned forward and dropped his voice to a low, even murmur. "I am going to interview you for this assignment."

Mark nodded. What else had he expected?

"I've known you for a long time, known my sister longer."

The two men held each other's gaze, neither blinking as their male language synced up.

"If you feel this way about her, and you have respected her thus far-continue. But I need to know a few things."

Again, Mark nodded and let his breath out on a slow exhale. "Shoot."

"If... and I say if... I stand down, will you stand up and take righteous care of her-wait." Wendell commanded, before Mark could open his mouth. "Care of her mind, her spirit, and then her body? Only in that order. Her heart?"

Mark nodded.

"Is that an affirmative, soldier?"

"Yes," Mark said clearly.

"Oh, shit..." Wendell sat back in his chair and rubbed his palms over his face. "I'm not ready for this either, dude. Dad should be having this discussion, not me. This all happened so fast."

Mark found a half smile coming out on his face as his friend's countenance relaxed. "I know, man. I don't think any of us were prepared... you know?"

"Tell me about it," Wendell chuckled tensely. "Does she feel this way, I mean, have you talked to her?"

The question made him hesitate. "Sort of, I think... I can't be sure?"

"And you need the time to tell," Wendell said on a long exhale of frustration. "But you don't have much time, here, but being here is jacking with your equilibrium, and you are trying to follow the rules-but being around her, with us in your space, is breaking your back and you are asking me to clear out..."

Mark looked out the window and then briefly closed his eyes. "Damn... it's that bad?"

Again he could not even think about how bad, much less talk about it.

"What if we go to Beijing as planned, and if me and Carol get a vibe that's correct, then we leave you to finish the last part of the trip together in Xi'an-assuming that Tina is okay with that, and this thing isn't a momentary burn like rocket fuel?"

"That's fair."

"Cool."

"Cool."

"That's all you had to say."

"Thanks."

"Thank me later... by doing the right thing."

"It's all good," Wendell announced, coming into the apartment first, nodding at Tina, Carol, and then Rita. "Mark's going with us."

"Hi, everybody," Mark said quietly, stooping for little Wendell to barrel into his arms, and without looking at Tina.

"Uncle Mark! You're coming, too?"

"Yup, buddy." He tossed his godson up and caught him. "Anybody else in here hungry? I'm starved."

All day he'd kept his distance, kept the children between them, flanked by Rita and Carol, with Wendell walking point. Architecture and shops and monuments had never been so boring to him. He walked by them, trying his best to simply make his godson laugh and to keep up a pleasant patter of conversation with his adult prison guards. It didn't help that Tina was so quiet, only giving him glances from the corner of her eye and a smile from time to time. As they stood as a whole platoon in formation at the airport, he suddenly realized that time had taken a mischievous turn.

He glanced at her, and for the first time in the day, his eyes held hers. Time was the one playing games-speeding itself up when their gazes connected and slowing itself down to drag the day along. It had rushed them to feel the way that they did, but then slowed down to a crawl for them to explore it-alone. And yet time was going to mess with him again in the airport and on the plane, seating him right next to her so they could talk for a short time, but then would rip her away from him again in short order, surrounding her with chaperones where there just wouldn't be time.

The tips of her fingers had started tingling as she'd sat next to him, and now the tension in her stomach fluttered like the Red Flags that the travel guides showed blowing over Tiananmen Square. She hadn't been able to really look him in the face all day, because if their eyes met, how she felt would have been written all over her face. Her hand had ached to slip into his on the flight, and the air between them had become so thick you could nearly see it. That must have been what stilted their conversation, she mused. They were both obviously feeling it. Sitting beside him created a bubble of anticipation that kept getting pierced by family interjections, children's questions and laughter, and the official business of traveling.

Without fanfare, they arrived at the Beijing Hotel in sight of Tiananmen Square. It didn't matter to Tina that it had housed countless foreign delegations, had old-fashioned splendor or that it was where longtime premier Zhou Enlai had stayed. The lodging represented both a haven and pure stress. It was where she'd be able to slip away to the quiet sanctuary of her own thoughts. But it would also be two rooms down from her brother and his wife, Rita and the kids, and a room that she could not enter. Pure stress.

"So, we all wash up, take a quick breather, and find a good place for dinner?"

Mark looked at Wendell, responded to his question as pleasantly as he could under the circumstances. "Cool."

"We could have dinner at The Golden Cat," Carol offered, her glances shooting between Mark and Tina. "It's Beijing's premier dumpling restaurant-and you like dumplings, right, Tina?"

"Uh, huh… That's cool."

"They have over thirty varieties, and we can sit outside to eat-they're open twenty-four hours."

"Uh, huh."

Wendell and Carol gave each other a look. Mark wasn't sure what it meant, because his primary focus had been on Tina, and again she was holding his gaze in a way that would make him soon need to look away.

"C'mon, Wennie," Rita quipped. "Let's get you, me, and Eva settled in our room, and Mommy and Daddy can get settled in theirs… and, uh, Uncle Mark… and Aunt Tina can each go to theirs. We need to wash up, all right?"

Tina glanced at Rita when she'd spoken and the bellman had come to assist the large group. She'd semi-noticed the way Rita had glanced between Wendell and Carol before she began moving in a nervous, jerky manner-but that was only from her peripheral vision. She swallowed hard. Her mouth kept going dry. She needed to find something other than the depths of his intense, dark brown eyes to fix upon as a reference point, lest she lose her balance.

The elevator ride up was making him feel like a caged panther. He needed space, and needed it now. The doors opened, and it took all the restraint he could muster to do the ushering thing. As each member of the group peeled away, each taking one of the rooms in the hallway row they'd been assigned, he tipped the eager bellman and glanced down the hall. Tina stood there with her card key, waiting on the bellman to finish with the others first. It was the look on her face that held him for ransom. Two doors down... two and a half days... just two doors down. He studied the numbers on his door as a diversion, needing something abstract to carve the image of her out of his mind. They would eat. They would get the children all settled in. They could go for a drink... maybe. They could talk... maybe. God help him, just two doors down, and not a prayer of a chance. Forget it.

OTHER GENESIS TITLES

A Dangerous Deception	J.M. Jeffries	**$8.95**
A Dangerous Love	J.M. Jeffries	**$8.95**
After the Vows (Summer Anthology)	Leslie Esdaile	**$10.95**
	T.T. Henderson	
	Jacquelin Thomas	
Again My Love	Kayla Perrin	**$10.95**
A Lighter Shade of Brown	Vicki Andrews	**$8.95**
All I Ask	Barbara Keaton	**$8.95**
A Love to Cherish	Beverly Clark	**$8.95**
Ambrosia	T.T. Henderson	**$8.95**
And Then Came You	Dorothy Love	**$8.95**
Best of Friends	Natalie Dunbar	**$8.95**
Bound by Love	Beverly Clark	**$8.95**
Breeze	Robin Hampton	**$10.95**
Cajun Heat	Charlene Berry	**$8.95**
Careless Whispers	Rochelle Alers	**$8.95**
Caught in a Trap	Andree Michele	**$8.95**
Chances	Pamela Leigh Starr	**$8.95**
Dark Embrace	Crystal Wilson Harris	**$8.95**
Dark Storm Rising	Chinelu Moore	**$10.95**
Eve's Prescription	Edwinna Martin Arnold	**$8.95**
Everlastin' Love	Gay G. Gunn	**$8.95**
Gentle Yearning	Rochelle Alers	**$10.95**
Glory of Love	Sinclair LeBeau	**$10.95**
Illusions	Pamela Leigh Starr	**$8.95**
Indiscretions	Donna Hill	**$8.95**

Interlude	*Donna Hill*	*$8.95*
Intimate Intentions	*Angie Daniels*	*$8.95*
Kiss or Keep	*Debra Phillips*	*$8.95*
Love Always	*Mildred E. Riley*	*$10.95*
Love Unveiled	*Gloria Green*	*$10.95*
Love's Deception	*Charlene Berry*	*$10.95*
Mae's Promise	*Melody Walcott*	*$8.95*
Midnight Clear (Anthology)	*Leslie Esdaile*	*$10.95*
	Gwynne Forster	
	Carmen Green	
	Monica Jackson	
Midnight Magic	*Gwynne Forster*	*$8.95*
Midnight Peril	*Vicki Andrews*	*$10.95*
Naked Soul	*Gwynne Forster*	*$8.95*
No Regrets	*Mildred E. Riley*	*$8.95*
Nowhere to Run	*Gay G. Gunn*	*$10.95*
Passion	*T.T. Henderson*	*$10.95*
Past Promises	*Jahmel West*	*$8.95*
Path of Fire	*T.T. Henderson*	*$8.95*
Picture Perfect	*Reon Carter*	*$8.95*
Pride & Joi	*Gay G. Gunn*	*$8.95*
Quiet Storm	*Donna Hill*	*$10.95*
Reckless Surrender	*Rochelle Alers*	*$8.95*
Rendezvous with Fate	*Jeanne Sumerix*	*$8.95*
Rooms of the Heart	*Donna Hill*	*$8.95*
Shades of Desire	*Monica White*	*$8.95*
Sin	*Crystal Rhodes*	*$8.95*
So Amazing	*Sinclair LeBeau*	*$8.95*

You may order on-line at www.genesis-press.com, by phone at 1-888-463-4461, or mail the order-form in the back of this book.

Love Spectrum Romance

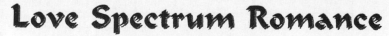

Romance across the culture lines

ORDER FORM

Mail to: Genesis Press, Inc.
315 3rd Avenue North
Columbus, MS 39701

Name _____

Address _____

City/State _____ Zip _____

Telephone _____

Ship to (if different from above)

Name _____

Address _____

City/State _____ Zip _____

Telephone _____

Qty.	Author	Title	Price	Total

Use this order form, or call 1-888-INDIGO-1	**Total for books** _____
	Shipping and handling: $5 first two books, $1 each additional book _____
	Total S & H _____
	Total amount enclosed _____
	Mississippi residents add 7% sales tax